I0580382

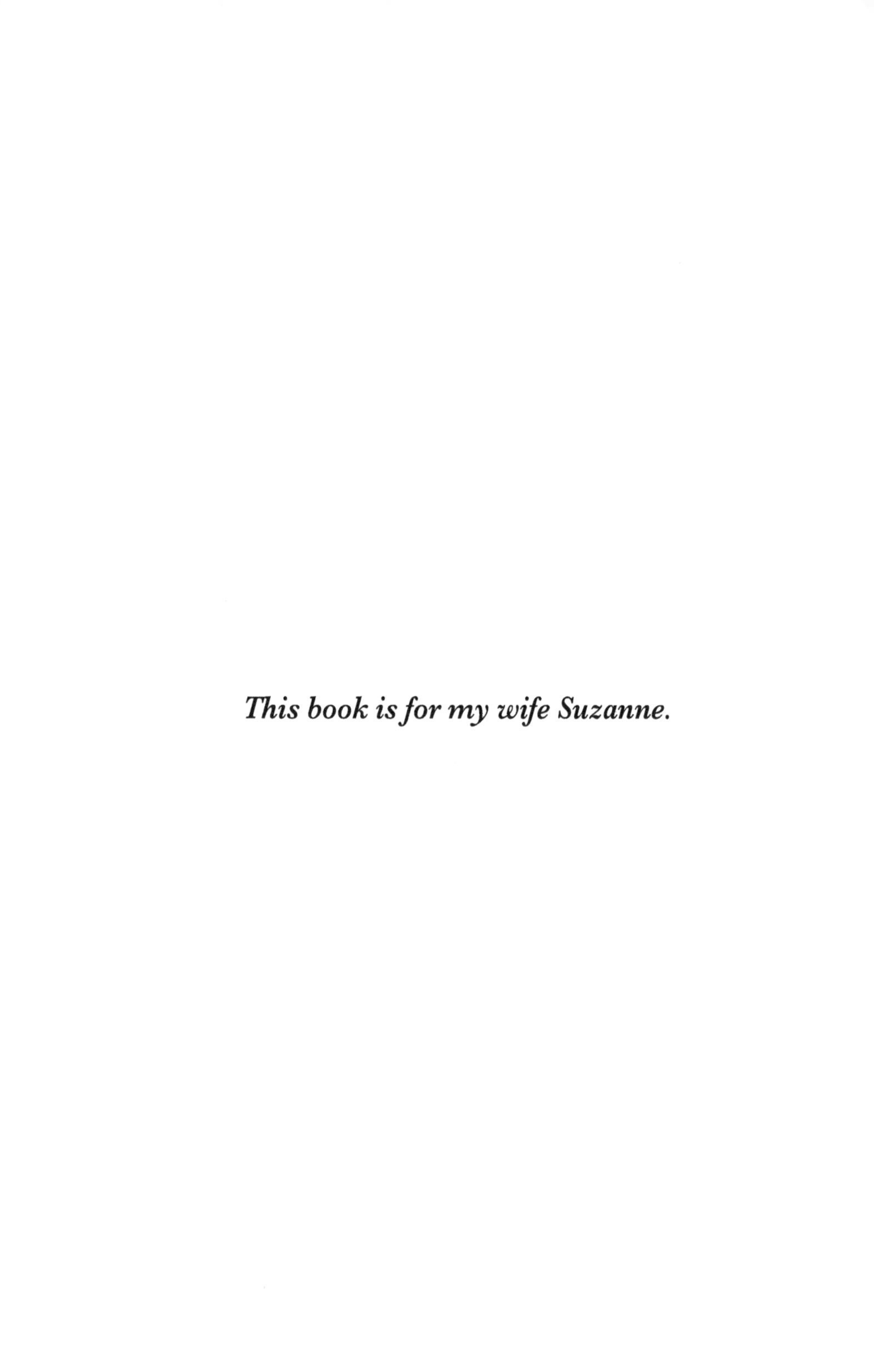

This book is for my wife Suzanne.

MYSTERY AT THE MINERVA CLUB

Frank Sutherland Davidson

OTHER BOOKS BY FRANK DAVIDSON

Frank Davidson is a graduate of the University of New England. Before concentrating on writing he had a career in teacher education at Sydney Teachers' College and Sydney University.

He is now a full-time writer of plays, short stories and novels. Recent works include "Bush Dreaming And Other Plays" [ISBN: 978-1-925909-02-9], a lighthearted crime novel "The Coral Airlines Mystery" [ISBN: 978-1-4931-0186-3], and the first of his mystery series "Mystery At Melon Flats" [ISBN: 978-1-925909-04-3].

AUTHOR'S DISCLAIMER

Although certain historical events are alluded to in this narrative, the author wants to make it clear that these are not necessarily presented with historical accuracy.

MYSTERY AT THE MINERVA CLUB

by

Frank Sutherland Davidson

PEGASUS PUBLISHING

Frank Sutherland Davidson

Mystery At The Minerva Club

First Published in Australia in 2024

by
Frank Sutherland Davidson (1934)

Orders: pegasuspublishing@iinet.net.au

PO Box 980, Edgecliff, NSW, 2027

A CIP catalogue record for this book is available from the National Library of Australia.

ISBN: 978-1-925909-15-9

Printed on Demand by Ingram Lightning Source
www.ingramspark.com

Contents

Frank Sutherland Davidson

CHAPTER 1

A *Curious Invitation*

It was just a coincidence that they both arrived at the lift at the same time – a youngish man, casually dressed in a grey tweed suit, and a young woman. He noticed that her hair was dark blonde. She was wearing a stylish cocktail frock in a sort of turquoise silk material. Classy, he thought.

He was pressing the button for the eleventh floor.

"Can I press one of the up buttons for you?" he asked her. His hand was hovering over the indicator, which was now showing the lift slowly descending towards them on the ground floor.

She looked at him coolly and was slow to answer.

"No – I don't think so, thank you," she said. "I happen to be going to level eleven, which you've already ordered."

"Oh!" he exclaimed. "Don't tell me we're going to the same place?"

"Well, the same floor, apparently," she said, in a tone that while not actually dismissive did not sound encouraging. He wasn't discouraged though.

"I've been invited to dinner," he told her, smiling. "That's the only reason I'd be going to the Minerva Club," he said, "seeing that it's a women only club, I believe."

She received the information in silence. The lift arrived and its doors slowly opened. He gestured politely for her to enter.

She did so, and as he followed her into the lift she gave him a carefully appraising look. "Well," she said, "I'm going to dinner at the Minerva Club too, if that's where you're going."

"Oh! Are you!" he exclaimed. "I'd never heard of it. What's it like?"

"I really don't know," she replied, as the lift began to ascend. "I'm not a member, and I've never been here before."

He smiled again. "Let me guess," he said. "You've been invited to dinner by your favourite aunt, who wants to find out all about the sort of life you're leading, and give you the benefit of her advice."

His manner was so pleasant that she couldn't help smiling back.

"You could be right," she said. "But the fact is, I don't know who's invited me, except that she's a club member."

He gave an involuntary start. His smile disappeared.

They rode on in silence until he spoke. "That's odd," he said. "That's exactly the sort of invitation I got. Not even a name to identify who'd sent it. Did yours come in the post too?"

"It did," she replied. The lift stopped and the doors slowly opened.

"I brought my invitation with me," he said. "Did you?"

"No." She stepped out and looked at the door facing them. The Minerva Club, it proclaimed. Members only.

"Please," he said, stepping out after her. "Have a look. Is this the same as yours?" He was unfolding something from the pocket of his jacket. She took the proffered piece of paper and looked at it.

You are invited to dinner at the Minerva Club …

She scanned the document quickly and handed it back to him.

"This looks the same as what I got," she said. Although she was finding this disturbing she kept her outwardly cool composure.

"Somebody's idea of a joke, I expect," she said lightly.

"But why?" he replied. Since leaving the lift, they hadn't moved. "Why?" he repeated. "We've never met each other, have we?"

"Certainly not, until now," she said. Although she looked calm and composed, she was actually at a loss, unsure of what to do with this extraordinary situation.

"My name's Jake," he told her. "Jake Pitlochry."

"Look," she said. "I'm going inside to sort this out. I don't know what you want to do, but I'm not going to do anything till I find out what this is about. This is a women's club. They'll have a register of members, and I'm going to ask to see it."

"Well," he said, "seeing that we've got the same invitation, do you mind if I come in with you? This is something I'd like to get to the bottom of. As I guess you would, too. "But," he added, "I doubt whether they'll agree to letting you see a register of their members. Especially if you're not a member yourself."

She scanned his face. Was he a part of the puzzle? Was there a hoax somewhere? Could she – should she – trust this stranger? Somehow his bewilderment seemed possible to believe.

"All right," she said. "Let's join forces." Privately she thought, two heads are better than one. "And my name's Cassie," she told him. "Cassie Wheatly."

"And you're absolutely sure you don't know why you've been sent this invitation?" he asked her.

"I've already answered that question," she said. "What are you, some sort of private detective, looking for business?" She knew it sounded rude, and immediately regretted saying it.

"Look," he said. "As I see it, somewhere in here is a member of the Minerva Club who must think she's got some sort of a link. To you, and to me. Whoever it is must think that, for us both to have got this invitation."

"That's a pretty big presumption," she said. "I'd prefer to find out who this woman is, before I begin inventing her life story."

He grinned ruefully. "I guess you're right," he said. "I'm always looking for an angle to hang a story on. Sometimes it gets in the way of the real thing."

She looked at him curiously. "What do you mean, hang a story on?" she asked.

"Well," he said, looking down at the floor as though he didn't want to meet her searching gaze, "I do a bit of writing."

Suddenly she understood. "If you do a bit of writing, you must be a writer. Is that your job, is it?"

He raised his head, and his eyes met hers. "No," he said, "it isn't. I'm a clerk in the head office of the Main Roads Board. That's how I earn my living. But –" He paused.

"Do you write stuff in your spare time," she asked.

"Yep," he said. "But that's not going to interfere with getting to the bottom of this funny invitation," he added quickly.

"Before we go in, let me have another look at your invitation," she said. "It was really stupid of me not to have brought mine."

He handed it over. This time she read it aloud.

"You are invited to dinner at The Minerva Club, Castlereagh Street, Sydney, at 6.30pm on Wednesday 19th October. On arrival, make yourself known at Reception on the 11th floor and you will be directed to the Club's private dining room, where your hostess will be waiting to receive you."

"Yes," she said. "Exactly the same as mine. Word for word."

As Cassie returned the invitation to Jake, behind them the lift arrived back on the eleventh floor and its doors slowly opened. There were two people inside. A dark exotic-looking woman and a middle-aged man. The woman was speaking.

"And how do I know that what you tell me, what you say, that you have the mysterious invitation to dinner here like I also receive by post at my hotel, but it is true?" she was saying to the man, in an accent that sounded to Jake like some sort of European but he couldn't place it exactly. Not French – that was for sure – but what?

Glaring at her companion in the lift, the woman added ominously, "not always, I find in life, that what the man have to say, it is what is true."

The man shook his head. "You can believe whatever you choose to believe," he replied in a weary tone of voice. "For instance, if you can believe that this is the eleventh floor, where you say you are going too, you could get out. I certainly intend to." And with that, both of them stepped out of the lift at the same time and moved in the direction of the Minerva Club door.

Jake and Cassie both stared after them.

"This Minerva Club," the woman was saying. "It is for women only, no? I have looked it up, it is told to everyone on the internet, where I find all details, and I know. So for what do you come here? You will not be wanted."

"My mother was a member here. There are current members that I know," the man replied patiently. "And obviously one of them has invited me to come and have dinner with her. Though why she should have invited you, it would be difficult to say."

"All will be revealed," said the woman. She knocked sharply on the door. The man laughed. "No-one will hear that," he said. "You have to go in and walk down the corridor to the reception desk."

"You," said the woman. "You open."

"All right," the man replied with exaggerated courtesy. "I open. You go in."

During this interchange, Jake had walked up behind the couple. Cassie had followed him. As the man opened the door, Jake said, "Excuse me, sir, but we're also going to the Minerva Club." He turned and indicated Cassie. "Do you mind if we come in with you?"

At this, the woman with the foreign accent turned around and gave Jake a scathing look.

"You," she said. "Another man. You will not be wanted here."

It was Cassie who intervened.

"I know this might sound weird," she said to the woman, "but from what I can gather, all four of us seem to have the same invitation, to come here and have dinner with somebody who for some reason, wants to see us together. Even though we don't know each other," she added, giving the man a somewhat inquisitorial inspection. She quickly assessed him. Middle-aged, good clothes, a somewhat weary expression. Probably a businessman of some sort.

The man looked back at Cassie gratefully.

"To me, that sounds like a plausible explanation," he said to her. "I know that I for one am curious to find out why I've received this invitation. And," he added, "who has sent it."

There was a pause. Standing in front of the open Minerva Club door, all four of them looked at each other. Jake wanted to laugh – the situation was ridiculous. But nevertheless, it was actually happening and his already active curiosity flooded his imagination with possibilities.

Cassie broke the somewhat uneasy silence.

"There's only one way to find an explanation," she said, "and that's to go in and meet this mysterious woman. That's if she really exists, and if this isn't an elaborate practical joke being played by some wierdo."

The man laughed, and the expression on his face seemed to relax.

"Not the sort of thing to expect from a member of the Minerva Club," he said. "While my mother was alive she spent a lot of her time here, and the members were overwhelmingly professional women of high standing."

For some reason, the foreign-sounding woman seemed to find his statement amusing. "You see!" she shrieked, pointing at him. "Women only. Men, no." She beckoned to Cassie. "Come,' she said to her, "we will find Minerva Club in here and ask for member who invite us." And with that, she stalked through the open doorway and proceeded down the corridor towards what was obviously a reception desk at the end of it.

The man courteously stood aside for Cassie. "Probably a good idea if we cooperate," he grinned. She thanked him and followed.

"That leaves us," the man said to Jake. "I guess you'll want to catch up with your girl-friend?"

"She's not – "Jake replied, then bit his tongue and didn't go on. Instead, he said "All right. Let's try and find out what this is all about." Together, they followed the two women down the corridor and caught up with them as they waited for attention at the reception desk.

The receptionist, who had been talking on the telephone, now put the receiver down and smiled welcomingly at the little group standing in front of her. "How can I help you?" she asked them.

"You can help me," said the foreign woman. "I am invited to dinner here by a woman who is club member. You help me please by telling name of this person."

"Oh yes!" exclaimed the receptionist. "Mrs Granville-Smith's party. I have a list here. May I ask your name?"

"My name?" said the foreign woman. "I," she said in condescending tones, "am Baroness Radislavsky."

The receptionist searched her list. "Oh," she said, I do apologise for any confusion. Would that be the same as Mrs Ludmilla Radislavsky?"

The woman tossed her head. "Here in Australia," she proclaimed, "I do not flaunt my identity. My husband, the Baron, he remains in Monaco."

At this, Jake stifled what might have been a laugh and turned it into a discreet cough, at the same time noticing what looked like the shadow of a smile crossing Cassie's face. Did she after all know something about this woman? he wondered.

But now the receptionist was smiling at the man. "Mr Tremayne!" she exclaimed. "We haven't seen you at the Club for a long while! Welcome back!"

"Hello, Rita," he replied. "No, not since my mother died. I know that Mrs Granville-Smith was a friend of hers. I guess that's why I've been included in this – er – invitation."

The receptionist had returned to her list. "Miss Wheatly?" she asked, looking at Cassie, who nodded and said "Yes."

"And Mr Pitlochry, I think?" she said to Jake.

"That's right," he replied.

The receptionist rose. "The other two guests are already here," she said, "waiting in the small sitting room. I'll take you in to join them. Please follow me."

Soon they were ushered into the small room where two other people waited. One was a middle-aged woman, the other an athletic-looking youngish man who rose to his feet as the new arrivals were entering. A bit older than me, Jake thought to himself – probably in his late twenties, he decided.

The receptionist discreetly withdrew and there were no introductions. Before the silence could become uneasy, the man who had been recognised at the desk spoke. "I'm Nigel Tremayne," he announced. It was a sign for others to identify themselves.

"Hugh Fraser," said the man who had risen. "And this," he added, indicating the woman who had been waiting with him, "is Mrs Leppington."

"Thank you, Hugh. I'm Grace Leppington," the woman said, in a manner that was both quiet and gentle.

She remained seated and Jake took the opportunity to introduce himself. "Jake Pitlochry," he announced, smiling round the room; then Cassie also announced her name, after which Nigel Tremayne, with well-exercised courtesy bowed slightly in the direction of the foreign woman and announced, "The Baroness Radislavsky, visiting from Monaco."

"Hah!" exclaimed the Baroness. "For tonight, because we sit down together for mysterious dinner party, tonight I use simple first name." She paused. "Is Ludmilla," she added. "But where," she said, looking round the room, "where is hostess?"

It was at that moment that the other door opened and an elderly lady, wearing a dinner dress of navy chiffon adorned with a large ruby and diamond shoulder brooch, appeared silhouetted against the light from the dining room behind her.

She was an imposing presence. Glancing round the room, she looked keenly at each person as she did so.

"Welcome to you all," she said. "I'm so pleased that you could all come."

There was a brief silence. Jake looked furtively around the people assembled but couldn't read any reaction other than curiosity and surprise – although he noticed that the Baroness seemed impatient rather than puzzled.

Their hostess – who, Jake assumed, must be Mrs Granville-Smith – smiled warmly. "And now," she said, "let me introduce my friend, Rosemary Nettleford, who is joining us for dinner."

She drew to her side a woman who had been standing a little behind her. "Rosemary has helped me organise this evening," she said.

Again the imposing woman looked keenly around the room. "I'm afraid that some of you might have found the invitation a little unusual," she said. But," she continued, "there is a reason for it. Now – before we go in to dinner, can we please circulate and perhaps meet each other, so that perhaps we will all get to know each other a little better."

Jake noticed that in response to this statement here were dubious expressions on some faces. He couldn't help wondering – if, by responding to Mrs Granville-Smith's curious invitation, would some of the people here tonight be helping themselves out of some mysterious trouble? Or would they be running the risk of getting deeper into situations that they mightn't yet be fully aware of?

He moved over to be nearer to Cassie.

CHAPTER 2

It's A Hoax - Isn't It?

Rosemary Nettleford, a woman of substantial build, plainly but elegantly dressed, moved forward into the sitting room and clapped her hands. "May I have your attention for just a moment?" she said.

There was something, a kind of authority in her tone of voice that seemed to demand attention.

"I would just like to make a small announcement," Rosemary said. "You heard from Sheila—Mrs Granville-Smith – that I helped her organise tonight's dinner meeting. May I suggest," she said, "that before we move into the dining room and ring for the excellent dinner the club is preparing to bring in, when we are ready for it, we mingle a little here and exchange just a few details about ourselves? For after all," she added, "none of you have ever met before." She smiled. "I'm sure that will help to break the ice," she concluded, turning towards the people nearest to her.

Jake sidled just a bit closer to Cassie. There was something about Cassie's straightforward manner that he liked. If he was going to have to talk to some of these others, he thought, he'd rather have her included in the conversation. And now Sheila Granville-Smith was joining them too, and Rosemary was signalling to someone else.

"Grace!" she called, waving at the woman who had been introduced as Mrs Leppington. "Come and join us over here!"

Grace Leppington did so without hesitation, and as she joined the group, Rosemary said "Now you four, I am sure, will find a lot to talk about. I'll go over and join the others." As Jake watched her go, he saw that Nigel Tremayne, Hugh Fraser and the Baroness were clustered together looking a little warily at each other, but relaxing a little as Rosemary spoke to them. Jake returned his attention to the three people he was with and waited for the hostess to initiate the conversation they were obviously expected to have with each other.

"I thought," said Sheila Granville-Smith, "we could start by telling each other the most important thing that we think has happened in our lives – at least, so far," she added, looking at both Jake and Cassie as she said so.

Grace Leppington smiled wistfully. "That could be quite a tall order," she said. "I've been a widow for nearly three years now, so I feel it would be disloyal to my late husband to choose anything but the life we shared together. And yet," she said," there have been other things."

Sheila Granville-Smith laid her hand on the other woman's arm. "Of course," she said gently.

Jake was having second thoughts about taking part in this so-called dinner party. There was something distinctly weird going on, he thought. And how was he supposed to contribute to this stupid conversation! He thought back to all the girlfriends he'd known – but none of them had seemed to make any important change on the direction of his life. He quickly assessed the influence of his parents. His father had been away from home a lot, and his mother – perhaps to compensate – had spent a lot of her time with friends from a local amateur dramatic society. Any step forward he had taken, had been taken because of his own initiative.

He stole a glance at Cassie, wondering if she was feeling the same inadequacy as he was. He was surprised to see the look of deep concentration that was visible in her face. She seemed to be wrestling with whatever thoughts were dominating her reaction to the challenge they had just been offered.

Suddenly she burst out. "My twenty-first birthday," she said in a kind of agonized tone. Jake looked at her in astonishment. He couldn't help reacting.

"Why!" he asked. Then, because of the look on Cassie's face, he wondered if his question had been too intrusive.

Mrs Granville-Smith took Cassie's hand. "It was something you heard about, wasn't it," she said. "Something you were told about – something that you had grown up not knowing – until then."

Cassie nodded dumbly. Then she spoke.

"It was after they'd given me the most wonderful party," she said. "When all my friends had left, my parents sat me down and I think it was my father who said that they wanted me to know something. Something about myself."

Cassie swallowed and shook her head, as though to dismiss any impediment in what she was about to say. She took a deep breath.

"Yes," she said, "it was my father who told me. He came straight out with it. "You're adopted," was what he said. Just like that. "Your mother and I -- we adopted you. We thought it was time we told you.""

Silence fell. Jake felt hopelessly unable to say anything. But deep somewhere within he felt certain that Mrs Granville-Smith had known this fact about Cassie and had prompted her to reveal it. A feeling of resentment flooded through him. Was this what this so-called dinner invitation was all about – the humiliation of a group of people, unrelated except for whatever this woman, Mrs Granville-Smith, apparently thought she knew about each of them? Jake felt an instinct just to walk out and leave. But at the same time he felt that he didn't want to go and leave Cassie here, with such a woebegone look on her face and the prospect of having to spend the evening burdened by the revelation that he felt had just been tricked out of her.

Too disturbed by what had happened, Jake failed to notice the look of deep concern on Mrs Granville-Smith's face. "That must have been a very great shock," he heard her say to Cassie.

"It was more than shock," Cassie replied. And now Jake listened carefully to Cassie's response. "It really sort of −I don't know − sort of destroyed part of me." She paused. "I mean, I'd always loved my parents. And now, where they had always been in my life, there was − I don't know − a sort of black hole. They were still there − but beside them, in my mind, was -- a sort of chasm with no end to its depth. I don't know − a sort of unknown part of me."

Jake couldn't any longer conceal his antagonism. "You knew about this − didn't you," he said to Mrs Granville-Smith. "Didn't you," he emphasised, looking her straight in the eye.

She returned a penetrating look at him, to which he responded with an angry stare.

"Old wounds can be slow to heal," she said. "Please don't be angry. Yes, it's true, I did arrange this dinner − with the help of my friend Rosemary − to bring together people who share a number of connections. But I did so," she said, giving Jake another searching look, "not to cause harm or distress to anyone, but to offer enlightenment. And that, I hope, will be the outcome when the evening is over."

Although this did nothing to dispel Jake's resentment, it did add something else to the disturbance he felt. He was suddenly experiencing, he realised, a sense of curiosity. He couldn't help his imagination taking over.

"You mean," he said to her, "that all of us here tonight have some sort of connection with each other?" Impossible as it seemed, his mind was immediately active with possibilities.

Sheila Granville-Smith smiled at him gently. "No – not everyone," she said, "we don't all share the same connections. But yet, in a way, the connections we do share can bring us all strangely together."

Jake shook his head. This woman is an eccentric, he thought. She might even be a bit mad, although you would never think so to look at her. But now he was beginning to feel fascinated by the idea she had just introduced. The imaginative side of his brain seemed to be working overtime, telling him that there could be a great story to be discovered here tonight. And yet, he couldn't see any way that he could be part of it.

"I don't think I'll fit into your idea of unknown connections," he said abruptly. "I don't think I'd be able to tell you anything that's happened in my life that's been any more important than anything else."

Sheila Granville-Smith smiled. "Sometimes," she

said, "moments like that can come upon us unaware. Why," she said, "who knows whether such a moment may be just waiting to happen for you – may be, as they say, just around the corner."

This enigmatic remark, while it did nothing to change Jake's attitude, gave him an unexpected flush of excitement. Yes, he thought to himself, life is like that. Things happen by chance – our whole life is a pattern of unexpected coincidences. As he thought this over his hostility seemed to be draining away.

He stole another look at Cassie. Her face had settled and she seemed to have her self-assurance back. She caught his look and gave him a brief smile in acknowledgement. Suddenly, he realised, there was something about her that made him want to get to know her better.

Mrs Granville-Smith cleared her throat. "I realise," she said, embracing the three of them with an unexpectedly warm smile, "that this situation is a strange experience. Probably not at all what you may have anticipated when you came here tonight. And so," she said, "it's only fair that I should give you an idea of the place I occupy in this web of connections."

It was Grace Leppington who responded. "I would certainly be interested to hear more about that," she said.

Sheila Granville-Smith's expression was suddenly serious. "My story," she said, "will not necessarily relate to everyone. Everyone who is here tonight, that is."

She paused, and again looked keenly at the other three.

"My link tonight to everyone who has come together here is through a great loss that I suffered. Quite a few years ago now. It was the loss," she said, "of my only son, Paul." She paused again, as though gathering the inner strength she needed to continue.

Jake's mind was busy now, exploring what possibilities this statement might reveal. What would this woman's son have had to do with him, or with all the others? He glanced over his shoulder towards the other group, who were now deep in an animated conversation. That Baroness woman, he thought. What possible connection could there be. But now Grace Leppington was speaking. What she said concentrated his thoughts immediately.

"It was not just the loss of his life, but the manner of it,' she was saying. "Wasn't it."

Sheila Granville-Smith looked at her gratefully. "Yes," she said simply. "What happened, was, that he took his own life. My son committed suicide."

The two women looked at each other. It was as though some sort of unspoken bond had been established between them.

"I too have known a sudden loss like that," said Grace Leppington quietly.

"Yes," the older woman commenced, then paused. "But," she added, "let's not allow ourselves to be overwhelmed. And," she added, turning towards Jake and Cassie, "let's not forget that for some of us, there will be facts that come to light that will in a way illuminate our lives in a way that is new to us."

It was Cassie who responded to this statement.

As though choosing her words carefully, she said slowly "I'm not afraid of anything I might have to learn about my genetic parents." She paused for a moment. "If that's what you're getting at," she concluded, carefully watching Mrs Granville-Smith's face for her reaction.

Sheila Granville-Smith was full of reassurances. "Nothing like that is intended,' she said. "What I sincerely hope is that we should all feel enlightened, and yes, happier, when the night is over."

Jake had been trying hard to find a sense of objectivity in the middle of his conflicting thoughts. He said to himself, either this woman is having herself on, in a big way, or there is something at the bottom of it that maybe – just maybe – could be important. But how could it be important for everyone? This group of six unlikely people, brought together by what seemed like an eccentric old lady?

Cassie broke the silence.

"I meant what I said. If you know something about my background that I don't know, I'd rather you came straight out with it," she said evenly. The remark was clearly directed to Mrs Granville-Smith.

Jake felt the need to back Cassie up. The sense

of outrage he'd felt on her behalf hadn't entirely left him. At the same time, he realised that heated remarks were not likely to improve the situation. He carefully controlled his voice before he spoke.

"Look," he said. "I think I can understand what you are trying to do. Somehow or another, you've stumbled across a few facts that have some sort of relation to some of us, and you've – I don't know – made a list, or something, to get the people together that you've invited here this evening. So that, maybe," he continued, "we might be able to maybe make new friends and find out something about ourselves, that is, something that you know, that you've found out, but that we didn't know before."

He kept to himself what he privately thought, which was, what business would it be of yours anyway.

"I think you've put that rather well,' Sheila Granville-Smith said. "Believe me, the connections you've referred to do exist. But," she added, "forgive me for saying it, but often the younger generations don't seem to quite understand what used to be admired as discretion. I think that facts which affect the direction of our lives should be carefully presented, to allow thoughtful assimilation. Why," she said, turning to Cassie, "from the way you described the manner in which your parents informed you of your adoption, I think all of us in this little group could understand the burden that the abruptness of that announcement placed on you."

A brief nod from Cassie indicated that she agreed

with what had just been said. "But I don't hold it against them," she said. "They had to tell me sometime."

"Of course you don't blame them," said Mrs Granville-Smith. "They are, after all, your real parents – doing the job that your birth parents couldn't – or, rather, weren't in a position to do."

"I do have to say," said Cassie, "I wouldn't have thought this until now, but it's been a real relief to have been able to speak about it." She paused. "To – let it out, so's to speak. It's something that usually I seem to keep bottled up inside me somewhere -- not the sort of thing you normally tell people about yourself. I don't, anyway."

Jake tried, successfully, to catch Cassie's eye. "It doesn't make any difference to who you really are," he said to her. "You're still you – the same you. Nothing can change that."

She gave that brief smile he'd seen earlier. "That's a nice thought," she said. "Thank you."

The incident with Cassie hadn't lessened Jake's impatience with what he still thought of as a self-indulgent eccentricity. He wondered whether, if he got the opportunity to suggest it to Cassie, he might offer to her that they excuse themselves and leave this so-called dinner party – he would like to take her, he decided, to have a proper dinner, with him, somewhere else. Just the two of them, and no hidden agendas like this set-up here at the Minerva Club. Getting the opportunity to suggest it to her was going to be the difficulty.

And it was undeniable that Mrs Granville-Smith was a persuasive personality. Look at the way she had drawn that information out of Cassie, he thought. And the way that both she and Grace Leppington, without even having a conversation about it, had unspokenly shared the experience of losing someone dear to them.

How had she come by these details about the people she'd invited here tonight? Then he remembered the other woman, her friend, Rosemary Nettleford. She'd been involved in making tonight's arrangement, he recalled her saying that. Was she some sort of private investigator? He knew that there were people like that. He couldn't stop his imagination from creating a scenario – two old ladies, nothing much to occupy them, get together and amuse themselves by delving into other peoples' private lives. What they find is a whole lot of stuff that creates a link between a group of them. And then, they decide to amuse themselves a whole lot more, by inviting six people who have never met each other, and enjoying the spectacle of revealing whatever they'd discovered about each of them. Or at least, that seemed to be the way the evening was heading.

It was then that it occurred to Jake that, if what he was thinking was true, then somehow, from somewhere, these two old ladies must have come across some aspect of his life that he didn't know about. He felt a quiver of apprehension. There had been nothing in his life – nothing that he knew about – that had been as dramatic as adoption or the suicide of someone close. Then why was he included in this gathering?

This is enough, he told himself. I'm definitely getting out of here. I'll tell this old lady that I'm not going to stay. I'll ask Cassie to come with me.

But before he could make the move that he needed to set this train of events in action, Mrs Granville-Smith had made an announcement.

"I can see that the others have had a very productive discussion," she was saying. "I think it's time that we circulated." She called across the room. "Rosemary, let's merge!"

CHAPTER 3

No, It's Not A Joke

Despite having his plan upset before he could put it into action, Jake was relieved to see the two groups breaking up. Maybe this would make it easier, he thought, to have a word with Cassie and ask her to leave with him to have a proper dinner somewhere. There were plenty of good restaurants in this part of the city, he thought, where they could get away from this absurd situation – and this pair of old hens who, for whatever reason, had created it, involving everyone who had turned up in response to their mysterious invitation.

That, however, was not how it turned out. Rosemary Nettleford walked over to the door that led to the dining room and pressed a bell on the wall next to the doorway. The door immediately opened and two uniformed maids appeared, each bearing a tray.

"Pre-dinner drinks!" announced Rosemary, as the maids began circulating. The first one held a tray that carried eight glasses of what appeared to be sherry, the second carried a tray of cocktail snacks. The first person they encountered on their round was the Baroness.

Ludmilla inspected the first tray. "Where is the wodka?" she enquired. The maid holding the tray looked towards Rosemary for guidance. Rosemary was not slow to respond.

"Ludmilla," she called across the room, "while we appreciate that at home in Monaco you might normally serve vodka before dinner – or at any time of the day at all, for that matter -- here in the Minerva Club we follow an equally old tradition – sherry before dinner is the rule here."

"Hah!" snorted the Baroness. "As much I thought. Here, no civilisation. No, no thank you," she said, waving both the maids on.

In fact, Jake noticed, nobody seemed very keen on the refreshments being offered and he saw with satisfaction that Cassie hadn't taken anything either. He could see that she was still giving all her attention to Mrs Granville-Smith, as though she expected the conversation with her to continue. Which it did, because, taking Cassie's arm, Mrs Granville-Smith led her over to where the Baroness and the man called Hugh Fraser stood together. Obviously by joining these two they were going to become a new conversation group.

"Ah!" exclaimed the voice of Rosemary, as she came up behind Jake. "You and I haven't had a chance to exchange a word yet. Perhaps we could have a chat before dinner." She beckoned to both Grace Leppington and Nigel Tremayne to join them. "We four," she said heartily, "might find some clues about what holds this group together."

Jake couldn't contain his frustration any longer. Choosing his words carefully, and controlling the tone of his voice so as not to sound rude, he said "It seems to me that the people who have come here tonight are victims of an elaborate joke."

As he said this, he noticed that Grace looked surprised, but Nigel's expression remained blank and urbane, as though he didn't want to be seen to have an opinion.

Rosemary gave Jake a look of careful appraisal. "I understand why you may think that," she said, "but it is not so. And I would have thought," she added, "that the author of a story such as *'The Gilded Fox'*, which was commended by the judges in the recent short story competition conducted by the *Inner-City Circular*, might have seen a certain potential here for the solving of several mysteries in which tonight's guests are involved."

Jake's jaw dropped. "How did you – you mean you –"

Rosemary laughed, but she did not sound unkind. "Oh," she said, "we have not undertaken this arrangement lightly. When I joined this Club, a few years ago, and Sheila discovered that I had a background in what I call forensic intelligence, she interested me in one or two situations that had impinged on her life. Problems to which she hadn't found solutions. Old habits die hard, and I couldn't resist taking an interest in them too."

"But how did you come across my story," Jake asked. "That one I entered in that Inner-City Circular competition? And what's it got to do with this – this meeting we're having?"

"Research," Rosemary replied briefly. "It's easy to find information on people if you know where to look."

"That doesn't do anything to tell me why I got that invitation to come here tonight," said Jake. "And," he added firmly, "that's something that I think all of us deserve to know."

"Well," said Rosemary, "this may sound obscure. But there is someone else here, one of the other guests, with whom you will discover that you share a special connection."

Jake looked Rosemary squarely in the face. "Unless it's something that you – and she -- " he said, pointing towards the other group where Mrs Granville-Smith was already in conversation, "something the two of you've cooked up between you to amuse yourselves."

"At your expense, do you mean?" said Rosemary. There was an edge to her voice as she said this that indicated hostility towards what Jake had said. She paused, but only briefly.

"For some people here tonight," she said, "the truth will be painful. As I think you may have already noticed," she said, looking straight at Jake. "But," she added, "please reserve your judgement. As Sheila has observed, more than once, old wounds are slow to heal. To which I would add, that when a light is shone upon a secret, that withers away its power. That's why secrets harm those who harbour them, and why this evening is intended to shine the light on several secrets that until now have affected the lives of people who have come here in response to Sheila's invitation."

"All right," Jake said. "Let's uncover some of these secrets you're talking about. Let's shine that light you're talking about and see what difference it makes to– to–" he couldn't find the words to finish what he wanted to say.

Grace Leppington finished his statement for him. "To all of us who have come here tonight, I think you mean," she said quietly.

In response, Jake could only nod his head. "Yes," he said eventually, "to all of us."

"Right," said Rosemary crisply. She turned to Grace. "You had a sister," she said.

Grace lowered her head. "That is true," she said. "She was a year older than me. I loved her dearly. I suppose you could say, I worshipped her."

"But you lost her."

"In several ways," Grace responded. She looked

the other woman in the face. "I can tell that you know what happened."

"That is so," said Rosemary. "But because it's something you don't normally speak about, and because you keep it preserved in your memory you are also preserving the pain of it."

"So do you suggest I tell the story of my sister here – now. To you, who knows it already, and to --" she paused while she recalled the names of the two men. "To Jake, and to Nigel."

"Put it into your own words," said Rosemary. "There will be a kind of therapy in doing that. Like the treatment of an old wound. Believe me."

Grace did not hesitate. "I idolised my sister," she began. "She was everything I wasn't – outgoing, artistic, the centre of attention wherever she went." She paused. "Maybe that was – I don't know – a problem, rather than a blessing."

"Because of what happened," said Rosemary.

"Yes," replied Grace.

Jake was listening carefully now. He knew instinctively that somewhere here there was a story being told. He couldn't stop wanting to encourage the telling of it. But he also knew that this story was something into which he shouldn't try to intrude. So he made himself keep quiet, and cast his eyes downward, hoping that Grace would continue.

Which she did.

She looked at Rosemary. "I can tell that you know all about it already," she said.

"I do," was the gentle reply. "As you know, only too well, I think -- it made headlines at the time."

"Yes," said Grace, "that was part of the trauma. Reporters telephoning, some even came knocking on the door."

"Wanting to find the background of the story," Rosemary supplied.

"Yes," said Grace. "Oh, I can still see every word of that horrible newspaper headline. 'Pregnant woman killed in car crash. Child delivered alive by roadside paramedics.'

"And that was the first you knew of it?" asked Rosemary.

"Yes - that was how I knew that my beloved sister had died," Grace replied.

Rosemary paused before asking another question.

"And," she said, "was that how you learned that despite the loss of your sister, you had a newborn niece?"

Grace smiled. But Jake, who had listened with increasing sympathy to the tragic story, could tell that Grace's smile was one that masked a deep sorrow.

"I'm ashamed to say," Grace replied, "that – at the time – the child meant nothing to me. Or," she added, "to my parents. They believed – and, I think, rightly – that my sister had been exploited and led astray. By a visiting Englishman she had met – admittedly a man of great superficial charm, and very good looking, but intent on nothing but satisfying his own desires." She paused, as though considering the matter in a new light.

"You know – " she said – "I've never seen it this way before. But – I don't know – perhaps he was what my sister really wanted. The charm—the amusement – the background – perhaps she really loved him after all."

"Yes," said Rosemary, "from what I understand of his background, he passed himself off as an aristocrat and held an English title."

"So we were led to believe, when we tried to contact him," Grace replied. "My father insisted that the man should be made to take responsibility for – for -- the child."

"And that never happened," said Rosemary.

"No, it didn't." Grace sighed deeply. "Oh, after the accident, he did turn up at the hospital, identified my sister's body, and claimed the child as his. But that's as far as it went."

"He never meant to keep her, did he," said Rosemary. "Too great an impediment to his self-indulgent lifestyle."

Grace sighed again. "Yes," she said, "and I suppose that's why he acted the way he did."

"Which was?' said Rosemary.

"For weeks we tried to make contact with him," said Grace. "Each time we were fobbed off by his acquaintances – people who he'd asked to cover his trail for him. It wasn't until one of them took pity on us and told us the truth, that we learned that the day after the accident, he'd put the baby into state care as an abandoned child and caught the first plane back to England."

"So," said Rosemary, "you couldn't have had any contact with the child – even if you'd wanted to."

"That's how things stood," said Grace sadly.

"Until now," replied Rosemary.

Jake noticed the look on Rosemary's face as she said this. It was puzzling -- seeming to show a mixture of emotions – sympathy, anticipation, yet with a certain note of caution. He couldn't help himself. "What do you mean, how things stood until now?" he asked.

"I mean," said Rosemary, "that one of the guests here tonight is Grace's lost niece."

There was consternation as the other three looked at each other. Nigel Tremayne's normally composed features suddenly betrayed confusion and alarm.

"Are you sure?" he said.

"How can this be?" said Grace.

But through Jake's head went only one thought. "It's Cassie," he whispered to himself.

CHAPTER 4

More Surprises

It was as though an electric current had passed through everyone in the room and shocked them all to silence. In the other group, Sheila Granville-Smith was the only one to move. Taking Cassie gently by the arm she steered her towards where Rosemary's group was still standing together. Jake tried to read the expression on Cassie's face as she came forward but all he could see was shock.

As Sheila and Rosemary then faced each other and exchanged a brief glance, it was obvious to Jake that the revelation that he had just heard Rosemary make to Grace had also just been made by Sheila to Cassie – and now, Grace and Cassie, strangers but revealed as aunt and niece in full view of this assembly of strangers, faced each other in the middle of the room as though each was uncertainly wondering what to do.

Jake felt embarrassed to be watching. Having everybody else silently looking on at what should be a private moment between them was wrong, he thought, and again he felt resentment about the situation he had unwittingly become involved in.

It was Sheila who broke the silence. "Cassie," she said, gesturing towards Grace. "This lady is your birth mother's sister." She paused, and then added gently "Grace is your natural aunt."

No-one moved or spoke and the silence in the room was uncanny. Grace was the first of the two to do something. Holding out her arms, she stepped forward to offer Cassie an embrace.

"Oh, Cassie," she exclaimed. "For how many years I have thought this was an impossibility. And now to find – that -- that my dear sister's girl – is – is here in front of me …" Clearly emotionally affected, Grace could not go on.

Jake carefully watched for Cassie's reaction. While she didn't actually pull away from Grace's embrace, she deliberately disengaged herself, and sweeping her hair back with one hand, said in a clear, steady voice, "please don't think me cold-hearted but I cannot turn my feelings on and off like a tap. My parents who adopted me will always be my parents. And if what I have just been told is true," she added, with a glance towards Sheila Granville-Smith, "then I will need time to – to take in something that I never for one moment ever expected to hear."

There was a brief silence. Then it was Rosemary, not Sheila, who responded to what Cassie had just said. "I can understand that it's a very great surprise," she said. "More than just a surprise, one might say. But I have certified copies of all the relevant documents and Department of Child Welfare statements, which I will show you – I think that will convince you that what Sheila and I have discovered, about you and Grace, is the truth."

"And," added Sheila, "I'm sorry that we can't offer to put you in touch with your natural father. But Rosemary has discovered that he was killed in Switzerland, nearly eight years ago, in a skiing accident."

Cassie stiffened her back, throwing back her hair in a dismissive gesture. Facing first Sheila and then Rosemary, with a quiet but firm voice she said, "I have all the parents I need, thank you."

On hearing this, Jake felt an instinct to move to Cassie's side. She needed comforting, he felt, and he wanted to say something to offer her his support. But before he could move, Sheila commanded the room's attention and made what seemed to be an announcement that was directed to all of them.

"I think." she said, "that we all feel the magnitude of this experience and I want to offer Grace and Cassie the privacy they need to come to terms with it." She smiled at Grace and Cassie, standing uneasily together, and said "let me show you into the next room. There, if you want to, you can sit down together, have a talk and break the ice that this unexpected revelation has caused." She moved to the door leading into the empty dining room and opened it. "Please go through, and make yourselves comfortable," she said.

Jake saw with relief that Cassie welcomed this invitation and he saw a brief smile cross her face. She and Grace shared a look of unspoken assent and moved towards the next room together. As they went into the room, Sheila shut the door behind them. She turned round and faced the remaining group. "You have seen the first of the revelations that are possible tonight," she said. "I would like to make it clear that there will be more. That," she added, "is if those of you who remain are willing to participate. I cannot guarantee that all the connections that remain to be made will be welcome."

On hearing this, the Baroness gave a loud snort of indignation. "And what is it make you think," she said, "that you tell me what I not already know myself? Pah! Is nonsense," she said derisively, glaring at both Rosemary and Sheila. "I am not ashamed of how I start in life. Go on – go on," she waved her arms about and was beginning to shout, "tell these people you invite here for so-called dinner party, but instead offer unsuitable refreshment, insult us, tell all," she gestured around the room, "tell all about how when still a young girl I learn how to make fashionable hats, how I begin to have clientele I satisfy, how I make my own millinery business. Of this I am proud. I am not ashamed, never."

"And why should you be?" asked Rosemary. "In fact – on the contrary, you have risen in the world by means of hard work and the use of your practical talents. I think we can all agree with you – you have an achievement you can be proud of."

"Hah!" responded Ludmilla. "You Australian people, you do not believe in the society of Europe. In Monaco," she continued, "there live many people who continue the aristocratic houses of countries where such distinctions, they are abolished."

"And in your case?" questioned Sheila Granville-Smith, as she looked Ludmilla squarely in the face.

Ludmilla immediately took on a pained expression and Jake wondered if she would answer Sheila's question, or just ignore it. He watched with interest as Ludmilla seemed to be struggling to decide. Finally, she burst out in an unexpected gale of laughter. "Oh ho ho," she chortled. "You want to know of my husband. The Baron Radislavsky," she pronounced. "Yes, it is true. I meet him because of my business. In Monaco, I earn reputation as milliner of distinction. I have many customers – even princesses from European royalties." Now it seemed as though nothing would stop Ludmilla from spilling out the facts of her background. "The Baron, he bring his mistress to see me so that I design and make suitable hat for her. "

Nigel Tremayne, who had been listening with rapt attention to Ludmilla's narrative, burst out in disbelief.

"His mistress!" he exclaimed. But Ludmilla was not diverted from her story. "Oh yes," she said, turning towards Nigel. "That one his favourite at the time."

"You mean he had others? At the same time?" Nigel gasped. "Always," replied Ludmilla. "Even now, I leave him to explore his fascinations. So I come on cruise to Australia."

Nigel had quickly recovered his usual composure. "And does the Baron expect you to return?" he asked.

For some reason, Ludmilla seemed to find this question amusing. "Ha ha," she laughed. "In the bedroom," she proclaimed, "he does not find anywhere the satisfaction I give. Oh yes," she added, "I will describe what he like, so you understand."

"Excuse me, Ludmilla," Rosemary loudly interrupted. "We do not need the details. I'm sure that we are all very pleased to hear that you have a life of − shall we say, a life of permanent satisfaction in Monaco. But we have other people here with unfinished stories. Although," she said, "you could help us with at least one of these if you would kindly answer one question I would like to ask you about your husband, the Baron." She added quickly, "nothing to do with his − er − his bedroom preferences."

Ludmilla shrugged. "I have no secrets," she said. "I have already told you all, and revealed all. Why you ask me to come here tonight, to me that is still the mystery."

"Perhaps when I ask my question," said Rosemary,

"it may become clearer. And now – if you are ready, let me ask you to confirm that your husband – the Baron – was he not educated in England? At a certain small but prestigious public school, where he was sent as a boarder?"

"What of it," Ludmilla shrugged. "That is not a question."

"No," replied Rosemary. "But this is. Was he enrolled there under his family name – and is that the Ukrainian name Koval, so that he appears on the school records as Ivan Koval?"

In the silence that followed before Ludmilla confirmed this information, Jake saw with surprise that a shadow seemed to pass across the face of Nigel Tremayne. It seemed obvious to Jake that the name must mean something to Nigel.

"Do you know that name?" he said to Nigel.

"Ivan Koval," Nigel gasped, as his shoulders seemed to twitch slightly. Controlling himself he quickly re-asserted his usual suave manner. Turning to Rosemary, he remarked, in a voice that betrayed nothing of the disturbance Jake had noticed, he made what seemed like nothing more than a casual statement.

"I was at school with an Ivan Koval," he said.

CHAPTER 5

A Very Big Surprise

Nigel's statement was immediately seized upon by the Baroness.

"Hah!" she shrieked, pointing a finger at Nigel and shaking it – almost as though she was poking a broomstick at him, Jake thought. "So!" she trumpeted, "you – you one of those horrible English who make life miserable. Oh yes," she continued, "the Baron, he tell me how you all exclude him from life in the boarding. How he is forced to enjoy more the talk with domestic staff, not you English snobbies."

"Indeed," said Nigel smoothly. "And did he happen to mention his frequent nightly visits to a certain maid's bedroom, after lights out in the dormitory? Did he go there only just to talk, do you think?"

The question did not disconcert Ludmilla at all. "English trash," she snorted, turning her back on Nigel and obviously terminating the conversation.

Sheila Granville-Smith was quick to re-establish a more desirable discourse. Going to Ludmilla, she placed an arm on her shoulder and turned her to face those who remained in the room. There were now only four others – Nigel, Rosemary, Jake, and the other young man, Hugh Fraser.

"Ludmilla," Sheila said, "believe me, we have no wish to pry into any other details of your private life. The fact that Nigel –" and here she gave a warning look in Nigel's direction, "-- the fact that Nigel went to the same school as your husband, is neither here nor there."

Nigel wordlessly accepted Sheila's rebuke. "I'm sorry," he said to Ludmilla. "It's just that at school I was an outsider myself – being Australian – and I can't help remembering how impossible it was to fit in. That was something that Ivan and I could have had in common – although we never became friends," he added.

Ludmilla inclined her head graciously in Nigel's direction. "You English," she said, "I do not blame. You have what is called the superiority complex. Most amusing," and she allowed herself a rather dry chuckle.

"May I remind you – Baroness," said Nigel, in the weary tone Jake had heard earlier, and giving her title rather more emphasis than was necessary, "that I am

Australian. Not English."

"Then for why do you go to English school,"
Ludmilla snapped. "To be made English snobbie, obtain
the superiority complex. That is for why."

Sensing the growing tension, Rosemary
intervened. "Nigel's father," she informed Ludmilla,
"held an important commercial post in a firm with
English connections. That was why he and his wife were
obliged to spend several years in London – years that
corresponded with Nigel's secondary education."

"Years that my friend, Nigel's late mother, enjoyed,
but that Nigel obviously didn't," added Sheila. With
a grateful nod from Nigel and an exaggerated shrug
from Ludmilla, the conversation appeared to be over.
However, for the first time, Jake heard something that
Hugh Fraser had to say.

"Well," said Hugh, glancing round the small
group remaining in the room, "I hope you don't mind
me saying it, but this has been a most extraordinary
experience." He turned to Sheila. "When I got your
invitation," he said, "I thought it was a joke. I couldn't
imagine why anyone would want to play this kind of
a joke on me. That's really why I came – curiosity got
the better of me." He smiled, and then added, "I don't
think there'll be any surprises in store for me. I've had a
fairly conventional life – no dramas, no scandals – pretty
boring, really."

Sheila smiled back at Hugh. "Yes, I can imagine
why you might think that," she said. "You're an only

child, I believe."

Hugh looked surprised. "How did you know that?" he asked. Sheila exchanged a glance with Rosemary, who nodded, as though to say – go ahead.

"It's a question of surnames," said Rosemary, emphasising the word. "Your Dad was Scottish, wasn't he."

"He certainly was," Hugh replied. "He never lost touch with his old country – in fact, he used to go back there regularly, to spend time and catch up with his old friends."

Jake looked up. "That's interesting," he said, "my Dad was Scottish too. He never lost his accent, even though he came to Australia quite early in his life."

Hugh smiled. "I think that would be true of most Scots who come to Australia," he said. "They never lose the accent – you can always tell a native Scotsman by the way they speak."

"So!" said Rosemary. "You two have more in common than you might think."

"What do you mean?" asked Hugh.

"Well," said Rosemary, "Let's look at some of those times that your father went home to Scotland. Did he ever tell you where he went?"

"Of course," Hugh replied. "He always told us that he was going to visit his home town."

"Which was?" Rosemary asked.

"Well," Hugh replied, "he said it was a place called Pitlochry."

When Jake heard this, he felt something like a cold thrill pass through him. He'd never known of a place that had his name. "What a coincidence," he heard himself saying. "That's the same as my name! Pitlochry!"

Sheila's face took on a serious expression. "What I am about to tell you," she said, "Rosemary only discovered by accident while she was examining some records that she had official access to in the Immigration Department."

Jake now felt a sense of uneasiness flooding through him. He looked at Hugh Fraser and was surprised to see on Hugh's face a look of apprehension that almost seemed to mirror the way he was feeling himself. It was then that he knew, somewhere inside, that he had to be prepared to hear some unwelcome news.

"I suppose you're wondering what Rosemary found," Sheila said. "It was this. A case where a certain man had applied for Australian citizenship but had been denied because he'd used a name that wasn't legally his."

Jake didn't want to ask the question. But he knew he had to. "And the name he tried to use?" he asked.

Sheila looked at Jake. "I think you've guessed," she said.

Jake swallowed. "It was – Pitlochry – wasn't it," he said. "That was my father you're talking about, wasn't it." He felt a savage emotion rising. He knew that everyone was looking at him. All the questions and uncertainties of his childhood seemed to well up inside him.

Sheila looked at him closely. "Were there some things about your father that you have always tried to forget, and yet they always seemed to stay somewhere in your mind?" she asked. Despite his reticence Jake felt himself nodding. "Do you want to tell us about it?" Sheila asked.

Jake suddenly felt what seemed to be an unmanageable and complex tangle of thoughts and emotions. He realised that the resentments he'd felt earlier about the strange invitation he'd received had suddenly been replaced. He realised, that suddenly, he understood what seemed to be its purpose. These two women – Sheila and Rosemary – for whatever their motive – had uncovered facts about the people they'd invited to this so-called dinner party, facts that they wanted all of them to know – things that life had hidden from everyone who were here tonight – until now. And he knew that, despite not wanting to talk about it, there was something about his childhood that he had always put away out of his mind. Crashing through his consciousness was the inescapable realisation that it was something that needed to be dealt with. And he knew that, unlike all the times it had surfaced previously, instead of ignoring it, this time he wanted to deal with it – and he wanted to deal with it now.

"I didn't like the way he treated my mother." The statement seemed to burst out of him. "Oh, it's not as if he was violent, or anything like that," he added quickly. "It's just that…" his voice trailed off. He couldn't find the words he wanted.

Now it was Rosemary who steered the conversation. "Would you say that there was a kind of remoteness about him?" she asked. When he heard this, Jake nodded. That seemed to sum up the whole relationship. "It was almost as though," he said, -- "almost as though – I don't know – almost as though he lived somewhere else, and what we had was only a temporary family. He was away a lot, too," he added.

"When he went away," said Rosemary, did he tell you why?"

"Oh yes," Jake replied. "It was always something to do with his job. He said they needed him in some of the interstate offices. Sometimes it was Melbourne or Brisbane – usually Melbourne, if I remember rightly."

"Well," said Rosemary, "would it surprise you to hear that it was neither Melbourne, nor Brisbane?" Jake shook his head miserably. He looked Rosemary squarely in the face. "Tell me," he muttered.

"He didn't leave Sydney," said Rosemary. She turned to Hugh Fraser. "And," she said to Hugh, "neither did your father regularly go home to visit Scotland."

There was a brittle silence. Hugh and Jake looked at each other. An incredible fact began to dawn on them, both at the same time. Hugh was the first to find words. "It seems," he said to Jake, "that we – we might have – the same father…"

"That is correct," said Rosemary briskly. "Angus Archibald Fraser, alias Angus Pitlochry. Now resident, under his own name, in South Africa."

Jake and Hugh stared hopelessly at each other. It was Rosemary who broke the silence. "If you want," she said, looking at them, "you can be brothers. The brothers that each of you never had – but that both of you wanted so badly. Half brothers," she added. "To be precise."

"Oh Rosemary!" Sheila exclaimed. "Must you be so pedantic? Brothers are brothers! That is," she added, "if they want to be."

Hugh and Jake face each other. Their eyes met. Hugh was the first to speak. "I'd be willing to risk it," he said.

The emotions that were flooding through Jake made it impossible for him to reply. All he could feel was that a burden he'd been unable to understand had been lifted from him. He held out his hand to Hugh. There were no words as they shook hands with each other.

"You two," said Sheila, "will have a lot to talk about. Why don't you go into the dining room, sit down together, and share what you know of a background you didn't know you both had? Until tonight?"

Although overwhelmed with the revelation that had just been made, and unsure of what would be likely to happen next, Jake followed Hugh as Sheila motioned them through the open door, then shut it behind them. In the dining room, Grace and Cassie, seated together at one of the small tables, looked up in surprise as they entered.

CHAPTER 6

Things Begin To Make Sense, Or Do They?

It was Hugh who spoke first. "Sorry to disturb you," he said. "But guess what." His excited joy was unmistakeable. "Jake and I've just found out we're brothers!"

Grace Leppington showed no surprise. "Oh, Hugh," she said. "How wonderful for you. Another surprise on a night of surprises! Cassie and I are still getting used to discovering each other." She looked fondly at her niece, who smiled back. "And if you two have discovered that you're actually brothers, it must be another relationship that has suddenly appeared here tonight. Brought to light by our – well, I have to say it – by our mysterious hostess. Just like the connection between

Cassie and me. We've just agreed, Cassie and I, it's been the most wonderful thing that has ever happened – to either of us. How do you two feel about it?"

Jake and Hugh looked at each other. Jake found, to his surprise, that he was able to put into words what he was feeling. "It's a funny thing," he began. "I've always felt that there was something missing in our family." He paused. A pained look showed in his face. "Well –" he continued, haltingly, "when I say – family – I suppose it really – really wasn't --"

Hugh stopped him by putting a hand on his shoulder. "There's no need to go on," he said. "I think we both know that the man who was our father – well – I can't put it any other way – he didn't have what you'd call a fatherly instinct. I know my mother thought that, I overheard her telling him that, one day, oh, years ago – when I was in my teens. Those were her exact words. Fatherly instinct. I puzzled over it for days, although somehow I knew immediately what she meant."

Grace Leppington looked interested when she heard this. "I hope you won't mind," she said, "if I just say that I have often wondered why some men have -- what you've just called it – a fatherly instinct, and other men don't seem to be able."

"I can't explain it either," said Hugh. He turned to Jake. "Don't you reckon?" he asked. "Is that what it seemed like, for you?"

"Well," said Jake, "it's something I've always had to put out of my mind. But I can only go on my own experience."

Grace was just about to say something, but stopped herself. She looked sympathetically at Jake.

"Is it something you don't mind telling us?" she asked him.

"Usually I wouldn't want to," Jake said. "Normally I'd want to keep it to myself." His whole mind seemed to be reeling. "But this whole set-up – tonight – I don't know –it's been so weird – it's as though – I don't know – it's like a curtain has been lifted – lifted on things I've wanted to keep to myself – but now – now I want them really brought out into the open. I want to acknowledge things that – well – that I suppose I haven't really ever known how to deal with."

Grace smiled. "I think that's true for all of us," she agreed. "But because of what those two –" she pointed at the closed door that let back to the sitting room, "because of what they have uncovered about Cassie and me – that we have a relationship that neither of us ever expected to find – I can't tell you what it has meant. To both of us."

"To both of us," echoed Cassie. She smiled at the woman who had so recently been identified as her aunt. "There's an old saying," she said, "that blood is thicker than water. And tonight – I'm willing to believe it."

"Good for you!" Hugh exclaimed. "I reckon that's how Jake and me feel too."

Jake nodded. "But I can't stop wondering," he

said, "what would have made him – our father – do what he did. What did he expect to find, in a family, and he couldn't? Why did he try to have two families – and just made a mess of both of them?"

Grace looked carefully at both Jake and Hugh, and then, in a quiet but definite voice, said slowly, "maybe he didn't know himself what he wanted. It's possible that he may not have known what he was looking for. And that might be why he couldn't find it – if that makes sense," she added.

"I think it does," Hugh said. "He always had this – this sense of being unsatisfied. I know my mother tried very hard to come to terms with it. I think she's a lot happier now, now that she's on her own. After he told her that he was leaving for good."

"He told your mother that!" exclaimed Jake. He shook his head. "It wasn't like that with us," he said.

"No?" said Hugh. "How did he tell you – you and your mum – how did he tell you he was leaving?"

Grace noticed the morose look that had come over Jake's face. She leant sympathetically towards him. "You don't have to tell us," she said, "not if it's painful."

Jake felt a familiar sense of anger boiling up inside him. The emotion that he had trained himself to keep in check. But now, he knew that he wanted to spill it out. He took a deep breath, thinking that he would control the level of his voice. Even so, he spoke harshly and the words seemed to shoot out as if they might have been weapons aimed at his absent father.

"He never told us," he said.

There was a silence as the others took this in. "You mean," said Grace, "that one day, he just went off and never came back?"

Jake looked at her. "It's worse than that," he said miserably. "My mother still thinks he'll come back some day. She's still waiting for him."

"Oh, that must be hard," said Grace. "To lose someone is hard enough. But to lose someone, and not know it – not realise that you've lost them forever, that must be a never-ending agony."

As he listened to what Grace was saying, Jake suddenly felt a kind of illumination. It made him feel that he wanted to thank Grace for what she had just said. "That's just what it's like," he said. "For my mother. It's as though she's living in another world – a world that doesn't really exist. And there's nothing I can say that makes her question it."

"Well," said Grace, "now you would have those documents that Rosemary must have discovered. The marriage certificate with Hugh's mother, for instance. I'm sure Rosemary would help you try to make the situation clear."

Jake gripped his head with both hands. "Oh my goodness" he gasped. "It never occurred to me before. If he was married to your mother," he said to Hugh, "then how could he have married my mother?"

"My guess," said Grace quietly, "would be that he

couldn't have."

Jake straightened up and looked at the others. A kind of lightness seemed to come into his manner, as though a burden had been lifted. "That means," he said, "I'm illegitimate! I don't have to be his son, and he doesn't have to be my father."

Grace said, again quietly, "If that's the way you want to look at it."

Hugh reached over and put his arm around Jake's shoulders. "It doesn't alter the fact," he said, "that you and I are brothers. I know that's true, and I think you know it too. And I reckon," he went on, "whatever you may think of him, we've at least got our father to thank for that. He's given us each other."

Cassie looked at them. "I think it's wonderful," she said. "That you're brothers, I mean. Something I always longed for, but never had."

Grace took Cassie's hand. "I think," she said, "that your parents adopted you because they couldn't have children. There must have been a reason."

"Oh, there was," Cassie exclaimed. "My mother explained it all to me. To be honest, I can't remember the details Something to do with fallopian tubes."

"So," said Hugh. "You'd like to have a brother." Still with his arm round Jake's shoulders, he said, laughingly. "take your pick."

Cassie laughed out loud. "Oh, this is absurd," she said. "Do I have to?"

Nobody answered this question but Hugh and Jake grinned at each other as they shared the enjoyment of their new relationship. After a moment or two, Grace spoke.

"Cassie, Hugh, Jake," she commenced. "Never in my wildest dreams could I have imagined what has happened here tonight. We four have been brought together in the most extraordinary fashion, by two people we have never met before. Never mind about why they did it, for us the result has been – I don't know – earth-shattering. I have found my dearest sister's little girl – now my lovely niece – and you," she said, pointing at Hugh and Jake, "have found the brothers that I think you have both longed for but have never had."

As she said this, Grace's eyes became moist, as though there were tears not far away. Cassie noticed. "Grace," she said. "I can't call you Aunt Grace, as perhaps I should – my mother would have insisted on it. But somehow – it's almost as though you are my sister, not my aunt – the sister I never had."

"And you," said Grace. "Instead of my sister who I lost, and grieved for so much, and for so long, I have you, her daughter." She paused, then looked lovingly at Cassie. "You have my sister's eyes," she said. "When I look at you – I see her." In a simultaneous movement, they opened their arms and gave each other a loving hug. Jake felt a warm flush – an overwhelming sense of gratitude flooded through him as he saw the depth of affection that Cassie had so readily discovered in her relationship with Grace.

It was Hugh who broke the silence that had fallen. "You two," he said, "You make a family. Even just the two of you. And believe me," he went on, "I've thought a lot about what it means to be a family. Ever since my father left. If you truly love someone, then that's what a family is. That's what makes it a family. People who love one another. Who can be true to each other, through thick and thin." He paused. "If you can't do that," he said, "forget it."

Jake wanted to say something but he somehow couldn't put his thoughts together. His mind seemed to want to go back to the emotions of his lonely childhood. Was what he was feeling now the same longing he had felt for so long while he was growing up, a longing for the brothers and sisters that all the other kids seemed to have? Was it a real family that he craved? He thought of some of the stories he'd written. He'd thought up some clever plots – that was why The Gilded Fox had won that prize. But he realised that in all the stories he'd written, he was skirting the truth that Hugh – his brother – had just articulated. If life is to mean anything, it has to be based on love.

"And if there is no love," Jake thought, "there is no life." It was an overwhelming idea and he seemed to retreat into a private silence, oblivious of the others.

The peaceful silence that had been established was suddenly interrupted by raised voiced from the next room. Hugh looked amused. "Sounds like Ludmilla is in action again," he said. "I wonder what she's objecting to this time."

CHAPTER 7

An Unexpected Crises

It was not long before the door opened and Ludmilla's voice could be heard loudly conversing in French with someone on her mobile telephone. Rosemary, taking Nigel by the arm, led him out of there into the dining room, followed by Sheila who shut the door behind them, leaving Ludmilla alone – with her telephone – in the sitting room.

Sheila explained. "Ludmilla is coping with a crisis," she informed everyone. "It appears that her husband has tired of – what did she call it? – his 'fascination' and has decided to follow Ludmilla to Australia, in order to persuade her to return to him in Monaco."

Jake was fascinated to hear this. His mind immediately began to picture the scene – Ludmilla, possibly at the airport, meeting the Baron on his arrival and deciding whether to forgive him for his wayward liaison, or to send him packing on the next flight back to Europe. However, his speculations were interrupted by Rosemary, who appeared to have been able to follow the French conversation and had more up-to-date news.

"I gather," she announced, "that the Baron has decided that he must have Ludmilla back immediately and has already arrived in Sydney in order to persuade her to return."

Jake's curiosity got the better of him. "Do you think she'll agree?" he asked eagerly.

"Well," said Rosemary, "we may very well soon have the opportunity to find out. The last thing I heard her tell him was the address of this club, and how he had to find the door to it on the eleventh floor. Apparently he's already in a taxi, and on his way here."

Rosemary and Sheila exchanged a look – Jake couldn't tell whether it was satisfaction, amusement or anxiety. But Sheila's next remark made it clear. "Even more that we had hoped for!" she exclaimed – and Rosemary agreed. "A stroke of luck, really," she remarked.

Sheila moved over to the intercom on the wall and dialled. "Rita," she said, "if a gentleman identifying himself as Baron Radislavsky should seek admission, please admit him as my guest, and show him into this room."

Sheila listened to the reply from the reception desk. Then she turned to Rosemary, raised her eyebrows and exclaimed into the phone, "Oh! Rita! He's here already! Then we shall expect him in a few minutes. Yes, show him in. Thank you."

Hearing this, Rosemary hurried to the door of the other room and called out, "Ludmilla! Your husband has arrived here!" Whereupon the Baroness stalked into the dining room and took up her position opposite the door to the corridor. Which was suddenly flung open, to reveal a dark, rather portly middle-aged man, sporting a prominent black moustache, who stepped forward towards Ludmilla and fell to his knees in front of her.

"Carissima!" he wailed.

Ludmilla regarded him disdainfully. "Do not speak your Italian here, Ivan," she informed him. "Like in all English colonies, here you speak only the English. And," she added, "get up off the floor. You are the foolish man. Why are you here."

The Baron scrambled to his feet, reaching for Ludmilla's hand as he did so, which she quickly withdrew out of his reach. "No, I do not forgive you," she informed him.

At this, the Baron drew himself up to his full height and swept his arm around the room, including in his gesture to all those present. "As your friends are my witness," he declared in perfect English, "I will never see Ariadne again – never. It is my promise to you, my one, my only. Besides," he added, "she has gone back to Greece and I am certainly not going there."

Lumilla appeared to give this statement some serious consideration. The Baron waited anxiously, closely watching Ludmilla's face for any sign of a decision.

"That woman, you tell me, she is a no-no, but can I believe?" she eventually declared, "and instead you decide to come to Australia? Most uncomfortable trip – unlike what I enjoy on board the luxury cruise. On which," she added, "Return? I may. Or I may not."

Rosemary, who had been looking increasingly impatient, now moved forward to confront the Baron.

"Baron," she addressed him, "although your appearance here is unexpected, we are nevertheless very pleased to see you. However, you must permit me, without delay, to present you to our hostess – whose name may or may not be familiar to you." She stepped to one side, allowing Sheila and the Baron to stand facing each other. Gesturing towards Sheila, she said, in a very even tone, "Meet Mrs Sheila Granville-Smith – previously Sheila Koval."

The effect of this introduction was to say the least, diverse. The most immediate reaction, and the most obvious, was from Ludmilla. "Hah!" she screamed, pointing her finger at the Baron. "More lies. You tell me, no living relatives. And now," she said, turning towards Sheila and addressing herself directly to her, "I understand why you send me invitation. You think, you have claim to Radislavsky fortune. What is left, that is, after he," pointing at the Baron, "spend so much on all his fascinations." For his part, the Baron simply looked amazed, and stared at Sheila as though expecting her to explain this unexpected news.

It was Jake who suddenly burst out with a comment. "This is fantastic!" he exclaimed. "What a story! Do you mean to say," he said, looking round the room at everyone, "that this lady – and this man -- are long-lost relations?" He turned to Rosemary. "You knew this all the time, didn't you! And that's why you asked Ludmilla here this evening. To get access to her husband. Who has saved you a lot of trouble by turning up here himself!"

Rosemary looked at Jake quizzically. "Partly right," she said enigmatically, "but partly only. Yes, it's true that Sheila shares her maiden name with the Baron. But that does not automatically indicate a relationship – as I think your situation, with Hugh here, shows us in reverse. You and Hugh have different surnames, and yet you are closely related by blood. Half-brothers in fact. Sheila and the Baron, on the other hand, although they may have the same family name, have no blood relation. The connection is what one may call a matter of historical convenience."

Sheila made a gesture towards Rosemary that clearly suggested that she wanted to speak. She immediately had the attention of everyone. "I think, Rosemary," she began, "that it's time all these good people were offered an explanation of the reason why we have organised this somewhat unusual gathering." As she said so, she turned her gaze carefully at everyone in turn. Jake noticed that when her eyes fell upon Nigel Tremayne, he shuffled his feet and seemed to be a little uneasy. An unusual departure from his usual smooth demeanour, Jake thought. But he didn't have long to consider this observation because everyone's attention now focussed on Sheila.

"It is a long story," she commenced, "so I hope you will all bear with me. In fact," she continued, giving Ludmilla a piercing glance, "one could say that it begins at the time of the Russian Revolution – 1918 or thereabouts."

Ludmilla was not slow to react to this. "Hah!" she exclaimed. "Do not try to, how you say, pin this on me. I am born Russian – yes. But supporter of Communist – no."

Sheila made a conciliatory gesture. "Ludmilla," she said gently, "we know your story. Rosemary has uncovered all the details – how your grandmother was abused by one of the revolutionaries, becoming a single mother, and how she supported herself – and brought up her daughter, your mother Irena, by working on one of the collective farms that the Communists established. And how your mother showed such a talent for learning the local folk dances that she was spotted by a visiting official impresario who offered her a place in a state folk dance company."

Sheila paused and looked sympathetically at Ludmilla. "Not the happiest of backgrounds," she said, "which may have prompted your mother to defect, while the company in which she performed was visiting the West – while they were performing in Monaco, in fact, to throw herself at the mercy of a croupier in one of the Monaco casinos, another Russian defector, who took your mother in and although they never actually married, became your father."

Jake saw that Ludmilla had turned pale. Her customary bombastic nature appeared to have deserted her. She was staring at the floor in front of her, but then slowly raised her head and looked Sheila squarely in the face. In an unusually quiet voice, she said, "I do not ask how you find these things. But all is true. I deny nothing. Yes, I do not know my father." She stared around the room, and continued. "He left my mother to take job in America. That is how I learn millinery trade so young – my mother sees opportunity for me, and puts me to it. That is life," Ludmilla pronounced, shaking her head. At last she held out her hand to the Baron, who grasped it eagerly. "And now," she said to him, "I have someone who still want to come back to me – even after all the fascinations. If I accept him, still I am the one."

"Ah," breathed the Baron in reply, raising Ludmilla's hand to his lips, "I cannot deny I love many. But it is you, my little sparrow, that I love most. Always, -- always -- always," he intoned, alternating his words with passionate kisses to her hand.

Jake tried to imagine Ludmilla as a sparrow, but somehow he found it impossible to match that idea with the well-established impression she had already made on him. And now, Sheila intervened.

"Ivan," she said to the Baron, "you and I have some unfinished business to discuss. Once again, I am going to rely on Rosemary to explain it all." She gestured towards where Rosemary was standing, and said, "please take over, Rosemary."

"I'll be pleased to," Rosemary said. "But, as Sheila has already said, it's a long story. Why don't you all find somewhere to sit," and she pointed towards the small tables, all with two chairs, that stood around the room. Soon, everyone had found seats – Sheila with Nigel at one table, Grace and Cassie at another. The Baron bowed Ludmilla towards one of the tables, pulled out a chair for her, and seated himself opposite. Hugh and Jake looked at each other, and then went to share the remaining table. Only Rosemary remained standing.

"As Sheila has already said," she commenced, "the story I have to tell you begins at the time of the Russian Revolution. And that means, it begins with Sheila's parents – who, as you already know, had the surname Koval – a name of Ukrainian origin." She was interrupted by the Baron.

"Very old name, much history," he pronounced.

"Quite so," Rosemary resumed. "And that history, that name, belonged to Sheila's Russian family – and had for generations, along with the noble title that went with it."

Jake was now deeply interested and could hardly stop himself from interrupting. How was it possible, he thought, for both Sheila's ancestors and the Baron's family to have the same surname, and not be related? He held his tongue, hoping that Rosemary's presentation would give him the answer to the question he'd wanted to ask.

He did not have long to wait.

CHAPTER 8

History Tells A Story

As I'm sure you all know," Rosemary began, "at the time of the Russian Revolution, what is now the independent republic of Ukraine was part of the vast Russian Empire."

This statement did not seem to find favour with the Baroness. "Hah," she snorted, "we do not require history lesson, thank you."

Rosemary was not offended. "Ludmilla," she said, "I am very much aware of your Russian family history. Please be patient, because what I have to say will concern you – that is to say, it will concern both you and your husband."

This statement did not seem to affect Ludmilla's dismissive attitude, but Jake noticed that a small frown had appeared on the face of the Baron.

There were no more interruptions and Rosemary resumed her address. "Round about 1717, when the Russian Emperor Peter the Great went on one of his fact-finding tours – which he periodically took throughout Europe, in order to bring his empire more within the European orbit – he happened to spend the night in a small Ukranian town called Radic. And while there, he heard of a local family – migrants from Croatia, as it happened – who had adapted their Croatian name, Kovacic, into the local Ukranian name, Koval, and were experts in the making of naval instruments, as the family had originally been in Croatia. This interested him as he was in the process of establishing what was soon to be recognised as a world-class navy. On visiting the family's workshop, he discovered that their latest invention was a depth measuring device, which if used on board a ship would accurately tell the captain the distance between the ship's hull and the ocean floor."

Rosemary paused and looked around the room. She noted a variety of reactions – everyone was interested, but the Baron, she noticed, was looking apprehensive.

"As you can imagine," she continued, "this would have been a vital piece of information for a navy intent on imposing Russian rule on the Baltic communities – what are now the modern independent republics of Lithuania, Latvia and Estonia – not to mention modern day Finland."

"Just so," the Baron interjected. "The Russian rule, made possible by the Radislavskys."

Rosemary smiled. "Not quite so simple, I'm afraid, Ivan," she informed the Baron. "It's true that what was then the simple Koval family benefitted from their invention. Peter the Great offered them an aristocratic title – the Barony of Radislavsky, as a reward to acknowledge their contribution to the Russian Empire – and a move from Radic in Ukraine to Moscow, to oversee the production of their ground-breaking invention, as part of the transformation of his navy into that of what was then the equivalent of a world power."

Jake couldn't contain himself any longer. "You mean," he burst out, "that the Baron here had an ancestor whose invention helped to make Russia a great naval power? Back in the eighteenth century?"

Rosemary looked carefully at the Baron before she replied. "That's what we think today," she said briefly. "But there are other events that have to be taken into account. That's why the Russian Revolution plays a crucial part in the story you are hearing tonight." She paused, as though deciding what she would say next.

For the first time, Nigel Tremayne looked across to the Baron. His look was not returned. Nigel stood up from the table he had been sharing with Sheila and spoke directly to the Baron. "You won't remember me – Ivan," he said, "but I distinctly recall being in the same history class as you at school – and hearing our History master – who had published a book on the subject – tell us that at the time of the Revolution a lot of Russian aristocrats managed to change their identity in order to pass through the border to the West – and that your family, the Radislavskys were one of them."

For once, Jake noticed, the Baron did not seem to be eager to respond. Instead, he waved his arm about and airily exclaimed, "oh, many people try to escape – some lucky, some not so lucky."

Jake was really wrapped up in the story now. "Hang on a bit," he called out from his table, "I can't make sense of that. If the family went out of Russia using another name, how come that Ivan here was enrolled at school in England using their original Ukranian name?" He turned to Nigel. "Koval, wasn't it?" he asked.

It was Ludmilla who supplied an answer. Despite gestures of protest from the Baron, she forged ahead with an explanation that seemed to surprise everybody. "His family," she said, pointing across the table to the Baron in a way that Jake thought seemed to be almost accusatory, "in Ukraine, his family," she emphasised, "Pfoof! They were nothing." She turned to point at Sheila. "In Russia," she said, with a change of tone that indicated approval, "her family, they were how you say, top drawer. Big estate. Too much money, important family jewels." She paused for a moment. "The revolutionaries, oh, very interested – they wanting to confiscate everything –" she then continued almost wistfully," including Radislavsky jewels, which he –" pointing across the table," – he has likely sold off to pay expenses for all his fascinations."

The Baron shook his head vigorously in response to this accusation, and the expression on Jake's face indicated his confusion. "I just don't get it," Jake said. "From what you said, it seems that one minute the family jewels belonged to her family," gesturing towards Sheila," and the next minute, they belonged to his." Jake pointed at the Baron. "That doesn't make a lot of sense."

Ludmilla gave a peal of laughter. "In this world," she said, "what is anything make sense? You tell me," she gasped, wiping her eyes.

At the table she was sharing with Nigel, Sheila rose to her feet. As she did so, her dress shimmered in the light and the brooch on her shoulder sparkled. Turning towards Jake, she said, "I can help you make sense of it – because, you see, my parents; yes, their family name was Koval, but their ancestors had been ennobled by Peter the Great; he gave them the Radislavsky Baronage. Over the years, each generation profited from their position and acquired much valuable property, including a set of jewellery which was worn by each successive Baroness on grand occasions, such as appearance at court. When the Revolution broke out, my parents had heard that they were in danger of arrest, possibly execution. It happened a lot. So under cover of night they left Moscow and made it to the border between Ukraine and Romania. Here they came across an itinerant couple, who had an understanding with the border guards at this particular crossing." Sheila paused, then looked directly at the Baron. "Your grandparents, Ivan, I believe." She stood expectantly, as though she had just issued a challenge and was waiting to hear it answered.

The Baron shrugged. "Quite possible, quite possible," he said, as though passing the statement off as not particularly likely. But Ludmilla had other ideas. "Possible? Possible? Only possible?" she said sharply. She stood up at her table. "I will tell you all," she said.

Ludmilla moved out from behind her table and with her back to the Baron, she faced Sheila directly. In the centre of the room the two women stood, facing each other, in what Jake thought might turn out to be a confrontation. However, thinking it over afterwards, he was struck by how they helped each other to tell what was essentially the same story, but from two different viewpoints. It was Ludmilla who began.

"His grandparents," she said, jerking her thumb over her shoulder towards where the Baron sat, "they have no real home. No native village where they belong. Their life, they spend it wandering. To live, they do whatever. That is why they have no real name – they are called in Ukranian language, Mr and Mrs Thief – because that is only way they can live."

At this, the Baron jumped to his feet and moved into the centre. "My grandparents," he said hotly, "they saw themselves as Ukranian and helped many Russians escape into Romania. They saved many lives. For this I remember them." His gaze swept round the room. "For this," he proclaimed, "I give them honour."

"So," said Ludmilla, "for the people who escape, what cost of this lifesaving?" She turned to address those still sitting at the tables. It was almost, Jake thought, as though those still sitting had become an audience waiting for a performance. Everyone was now watching Ludmilla. Her gaze swept round the tables. "Very early in life, I discover," she informed those sitting, as though taking them all into her confidence, "if someone have what I want, to get it I must pay." She paused. "Is called supply and demand," she elaborated. "That is how I make successful millinery business. For what I supply, I demand payment." She nodded vigorously. "In advance," she added.

The Baron quickly interrupted. "That has nothing to do with Russian people going from Ukraine into Romania," he protested. "It is true," he went on, looking around the seated listeners, "sometimes money changed hands. How else," he asked, "do you think the border guards could have been persuaded to turn a blind eye?"

At this, Ludmilla's unusual sense of humour asserted itself. "Ho ho ho," she chortled. "Not always money, I think."

As though sensing what seemed like a developing confrontation between the two Radislavskys, Sheila made a placatory gesture towards Ludmilla which interrupted her, and Sheila took the opportunity to resume the story she had earlier commenced.

"When my parents arrived at the border," she began, "they sought out the couple they had heard of who, it was said, had an arrangement with the border guards. Just as Ludmilla has said, it was possible to buy the anonymity needed to be able to cross safely into Romania." Her gaze fell upon the Baron. "They found this couple and sat down with them at their camp fire," she continued, "and commenced negotiation. According to what my father told me, all they had been able to carry with them from Moscow was what you have heard described as the family jewels – and the Ukranian itinerant couple had heard this. That was why the man made the offer he did – which was, in return for giving him the crowning piece of the jewellery collection – a ruby and diamond tiara -- he would ensure safe passage for my parents across the border into Romania – not under their own name and title, the Baron and Baroness Radislavsky, but as the Ukranian couple whom the guards allowed free and frequent access to and from Romania."

Jake gasped. "You mean, they changed identity?" he said. "They pretended to be – the – the wandering Ukranians – what did you say they were called," he asked Ludmilla, "Mr and Mrs Thief? And they got away with it – got out of Russia and into Romania?"

"Exactly," Sheila smiled. "Of course, in places like that, there was no photo identity as we have today – everything was done with documents. My father surrendered the proof of the family's identity and told the Ukranian to make whatever use he wanted of it – which, apparently," she said, giving the Baron a half-amused look, "he was not slow to do."

It was at this point that Ludmilla took back control

of the conversation. She turned to face Sheila. "You – and your friend," she said, gesturing towards Rosemary, "you are very clever women. How you find all details I do not know. But now I do know why you want me here this evening. Why you send me mystery invitation. It is what I suspect."

Ludmilla paused. She pointed over her shoulder towards the Baron. "In Russia, my mother tell me, we have a saying – and that saying, it is guide to a good life. I tell you that saying. 'Eat bread and salt and speak the truth.' Always the truth, it must be heard to replace the falsehood."

Ludmilla again pointed behind her. "What does it matter? I will always be a milliner – a milliner of distinction. If he will tell all what happened at the border – all those years ago, I say now – I will overlook any recent fascinations." She paused, and glanced over her shoulder. "Yes," she said, "If the truth is spoken, I will return with him to Monaco. If not – Pfoof!" she exclaimed.

The eyes of all the listeners – Grace and Cassie, still at their table, Jake and Hugh at theirs, and Nigel, left alone where he had sat with Sheila, now focussed on the Baron.

"Carissima," he exclaimed. "Must I?"

"Ivan!" Ludmilla exclaimed,

"Here, the Italian we do not understand. Here you must speak the English."

"My beloved," the Baron exclaimed in reply, "even after travelling around the world to see you, I will tell the secret my father told me, how he came to use the Radislasvsky title, how he rose in the world and became accepted member of exiled aristocracy in Monaco." He paused. "But first," he said, looking towards Rosemary," before I start, it has been a long journey to be with you tonight. A little refreshment would be very welcome."

"Of course!" Rosemary exclaimed, going to the intercom on the wall and picking up the receiver. "Rita," she said. "Ask them to send in a tray of vodka."

Ludmilla's eyes lit up. "Civilisation! At last!" she exclaimed.

CHAPTER 9

The Baron's Story

Soon one of the uniformed maids appeared, carrying a tray that held not only glasses of vodka but a full bottle – it was as though the staff had realised that some of the guests might require a refill. This was certainly the case when the tray reached the Baron. Taking one of the full glasses and holding it high, "Za Nas!" he cried, before downing his drink in one swallow and pouring himself another from the bottle.

"He wishing you all the good health," explained the Baroness, as she repeated the toast and also downed her drink without drawing breath. "Is good," she commented, returning her empty glass to the tray. "And now, Ivan," she said to the Baron, "you tell."

"Ah," said the Baron, wiping his moustache, "I have to rely on what my father told me. Yes, it is true, my grandfather had the ear of the border guards and for him, the Radislavsky tiara was unprecedented wealth. One jewel from the tiara was more than enough to guarantee the – well, I have to say their name – the Koval couple -- to pass through safely into Romania. They were free to commence a new life – not as Russian aristocrats, because they had given proof of their title away to my grandfather, but as ordinary citizens." He paused.

"I cannot deny," he said, "that my grandfather came from nothing. But when he saw an opportunity, he took it, and the Radislavsky tiara gave him an opportunity to change his life. Jewel by jewel, over the years he dismantled it to pay for a new life in Romania. And," he added, "that included an education for his son, my father – something that would never been possible without the jewels from the tiara."

The maid carrying the vodka tray had completed her round and went to withdraw from the room, but Rosemary signalled her to remain. Jake saw with amusement that this was obviously because Rosemary thought that more vodka might be required as the Baron's story unfolded.

Ivan was in full swing now – obviously, thought Jake, stimulated by the shots of vodka he had already consumed. "All my life," he cried, waving his arms about, "I have been obliged to conceal my origins." He turned to Nigel. "Don't think, Tremayne," he said , "that

I don't recognise you. I never knew at school you were an outsider like myself. I thought you were English, like the rest of them."

It surprised Jake that Nigel laughed at this. "Let's forget it," he said in reply. "Tonight we only remember what is important."

In her quiet voice, Grace added a comment. "Important for us all to help each other move forward," she said.

Jake noticed that Hugh nodded in agreement with this. Now Hugh spoke. "If we can put the bad things that have happened to us away out of our memory," he was saying, "that will leave more room for us to remember the good things."

Simple though this statement was, it seemed to strike a chord everywhere. "That's good thinking, Hugh," Grace remarked; and Cassie gave Hugh a brilliant smile. "That sounds like a path that could lead to a happy life," she said to him.

"A happy life!" exclaimed the Baron. "That is what my grandparents sought in Romania. But," he said, "always they were tagged with the description of their origins in Ukraine. And for my father it was the same. As he grew to manhood, the gap widened between what he came from and what he now was. The education he got did not wipe out the facts of his background."

As he listened, in Jake's imagination he pictured Ivan's father -- perhaps looking like Ivan in appearance – short, possibly pudgy like Ivan, with dark hair and a moustache – isolated in a culture that he wanted to belong to but separated from it by the experiences of his early years – the son of people regarded back in Ukraine as thieves and beggars.

"My father," said Ivan, "was determined to leave his Ukranian roots behind. According to what he told me, he learnt three foreign languages – in addition to Romanian – German, French and English. This enabled him to establish trading deals with foreign merchants, and he was able to persuade his father to let him use the last remaining jewels from the tiara to set up a trading company." Ivan paused, and wiped his forehead with a handkerchief. It was almost as though the weight of the story he was telling was using all his energy.

Rosemary quickly signalled to the maid with the vodka tray. She came forward to where Ivan was standing. "Ah," he breathed, pouring himself a generous glassful, "Zheezn!" He downed his drink and shook his head.

"He says you save his life," the Baroness explained, beckoning the maid over and also helping herself. "Now," she said, replacing her empty glass, "we hear more." She gave an encouraging wave in the Baron's direction. "Come, Ivan. Tell all," she commanded.

"Always used to being on the move, they had moved on," Ivan continued, "over the next border, into Transylvania, to a town called Varad. It was there that my grandparents died, and where my father fell in love with my mother."

Ludmilla felt obliged to elaborate this information. "His father," she said, pointing at the Baron, "for him, enough to love one person. Not like some other people," she said meaningfully, "with their fascinations."

The Baron ignored this remark and continued. "She was the daughter of a local landowner," he said, "a Hungarian Count, to whom my father's background seemed inadequate. And," he said, "that was why he took the step he did – by claiming that the Russian document that his late father had carefully preserved, was a document issued by the Russian court describing the family from which he was descended. It was then," the Baron continued, "that he claimed the name – Koval. The name by which he then appeared in the Church record of his marriage in Varad, in the British citizenship record which he later obtained in London, and by which he was always known – until his death in 1990."

Again the Baron faltered; but Ludmilla was not going to let the story lapse. "And with the name," she proclaimed, "also he became the Radislavsky – because his piece of paper said so." The Baron wiped his brow again. "It is true," he said, "my father assumed a title that had belonged to others. But," he added, "by then, all Russian titles had been abolished by the communists – so what did it matter."

Jake stole a glance at Sheila. What was she thinking, he wondered, now that she had heard the story of her family's loss of their Russian identity. But all he could tell from the expression on her face was that she wanted to hear more. And the Baron was obviously not finished.

"My parents did not stay in Varad," he continued. "By now, my father had built up a successful trading company – the income from which I still enjoy today." He paused and gave Ludmilla a look that was both tender and reproachful. "And which," he continued, "supports our life in Monaco. Not," he stressed, "the Radislavsky jewels. Those were all expended by my grandfather, as I have already told. And anyway," he continued, "the tiara was only one piece of the Radislavsky collection. There were other pieces – of which I know nothing."

Ludmilla accepted the Baron's implied rebuke with a grace that surprised Jake. She moved over to where the Baron was standing and offered him her hand, which he avidly took in his. "Despite all the fascinations," she informed him, "Ivan, you are my only love. With or without the Radislavsky Baronage, I am still the milliner – the milliner of distinction – who you found irresistible. Always," she stated, "I will be yours." After a moment she added, as though as an afterthought, "especially without any further fascinations."

Jake wasn't sure who started it -- thinking about it afterwards, he wondered, could it have been me? But, as the Baroness concluded her speech, from one of the tables rang out an enthusiastic clapping of hands, which was taken up by all those still sitting. The volley of approval was acknowledged by a bow from the Baroness, followed by a bow from the Baron as, hand in hand, they left the centre of the room and retired to the table they had previously shared together.

That left standing in the centre, just Rosemary and Sheila – the two architects of this strange and rather wonderful event, Jake thought. He also wondered if there was ever going to be any sign of the dinner, the promise of which had brought them together – the six invited guests, he mused, and now the additional uninvited one. As though reading his mind, Sheila spoke.

"Dinner will be served shortly," she said, "but first, a few moments while Rosemary completes Ivan's story. Because, there is more to tell, isn't there, Rosemary," she said; to which Rosemary nodded. "There is," she said, "and also, if I'm not mistaken, something that you can add from the experiences of your parents – who, you remember," she said to those sitting, "although having made a new life for themselves in Australia, were originally Russian."

In response, Sheila smiled. "Very well," she replied, "but I shall make it brief. And now – over to you," she concluded, leaving Rosemary alone in the centre and moving over to the table where she had previously been sitting with Nigel.

"Ivan's parents," began Rosemary, "the educated ex-Ukranian and the Hungarian Count's daughter --although very happy together, led a life in which their only child – Ivan – was something of an accessory, rather than an essential part of what makes a family. By the time Ivan was born, they were living in Vienna – with so many frequent trips to Paris and London that Ivan's father decided that they should move permanently to either one or the other. As it happened, application for British citizenship was the less complicated of the two, so that is why by 1988 they had settled in London. It was there, a couple of years later, that Ivan's mother lost her life – crossing a busy road, she had never got used to traffic driving on the left hand side of the road, instead of on the right as they did in all the European countries, and unfortunately she walked right in front of an oncoming London bus and was killed instantly." Rosemary paused briefly and gave Ivan a look of sympathy. "In a way," she said, "the accident that deprived Ivan of his mother, also deprived him of his father. Unable to come to terms with the loss of his wife, he enrolled Ivan in an English boarding school –the one to which Nigel also went later – and moved to Monaco, where he identified himself with the community of exiled European aristocrats living there. And, naturally," Rosemary added, "made good use of the Russian title he had adopted."

At his table, the Baron nodded his head vigorously. "Just so," he agreed; "and when he died and I went to Monaco to sort out his estate, I found an affidavit witnessed by an attorney saying that to inherit his assets I must also inherit – and employ – the title by which he had become known there."

"The Baron Radislavsky," supplied Ludmilla; although, Jake thought as she was saying it, by now everyone has understood the Baron's story without needing any further explanations. Rosemary turned to Ludmilla and smiled. "The rank to which you also became entitled when you and Ivan – as we say here – tied the knot," she said.

The vehemence of Ludmilla's reply surprised Jake. "What is not mine," she said, "I do not want." She stood up, moved from behind her table and called across to where Sheila sat. "In Monaco I have been the Baroness Radislavsky," she said in a loud and definite voice. "Here, tonight, I have become again what I was before – Ludmilla Popov, maker of hats. But also," she added, turning to the Baron, "wife of Ivan Koval, whether he is Baron or not Baron."

Now Sheila also stood, and again the two faced each other. "Ludmilla," Sheila said, "what is past is past. "The fact is, my father gave away his title –to which I might have succeeded, had he kept it – in order to buy the safety of himself and his wife, my mother. What has been freely given, one should not expect to repossess." She paused and stepped out from behind her table. "There is no question of me trying to reclaim the Baronage. While the title is useful to you and Ivan – which it certainly appears to be today in Monaco – you must keep it and make whatever use of it you will. After all," she added, "it has now been in Ivan's family for three generations. We cannot undo history." She paused, then inclined her head towards Ludmilla in a courteous bow. "I acknowledge you," she said, "as Baroness, wife of the Baron Radislavsky."

This was something that Jake had not expected and he turned towards Ludmilla to see what her reaction would be. That Sheila's statement had amazed her was obvious but, Jake saw, she quickly collected her wits and replied.

"You are very gracious lady," she said, in a tone which Jake thought of as humble; and then, much to Jake's astonishment, she executed a deep curtsy towards Sheila, signalling to Ivan to also make his acknowledgement – which he did with a deep bow. Sheila smiled warmly at both of them. "Thank you," she said simply; "and now I think we should do something about these seating arrangements, and ring for dinner to be brought in."

"Do you mean," said Rosemary, "that we should bring these separate tables together?"

"That's exactly what I mean," Sheila replied.

Hugh took the hint immediately. "Come on, Jake," he cried, "push these together – we can make one big table out of these small ones, if we put them end-to-end."

"A table for nine," said Rosemary, counting the chairs. "Four on each side, and Sheila at the head." Soon the furniture was re-arranged and everyone began to seat themselves. Jake noticed that Cassie and Hugh had chosen to sit next to each other. The sight of them together gave him a warm feeling; as though he was seeing something that was somehow intended. Grace noticed it too. "It is too early," she said to Jake in her quiet voice, "but I think that Cassie and Hugh might become good friends." Jake caught the underlying implication and a feeling of happiness flooded through him. He smiled at Grace. "I know they will," he said simply.

Rosemary had rung the bell at the doorway and

now the two maids wheeled in a trolley on which sat steaming plates of soup, which they began to place before each person at the table. Sheila smiled along each side of the table and waved at Ivan and Ludmilla, seated opposite each other at the other end. "In celebration of our shared Russian heritage," she called to them, "our first course tonight will be borsch – the classic Russian soup."

Ludmilla, who had just unfolded her table napkin, waved it in the air like a flag of triumph. "Borsch!" she exclaimed. "Nebesa!" She turned, waving to Sheila.

"Tonight, here at Minerva Club, in Australia," she called, "what I never expect -- I am in heaven."

CHAPTER 10

Sheila's Story

As the diners began to enjoy their borsch, Grace said quietly, "I never expected to be able to enjoy a soup made of cabbage leaves!"

"Oh," said Sheila, "there's much more to it than that. When I submitted the menu for tonight, I discovered that the Club chef had never even heard of borsch. I had to spend an hour in the kitchen with him, to ensure that he knew how to make it properly. We often had it at home, and he's using my mother's recipe."

"I've been wondering," said Jake, "when your parents left Russia, what made them decide to come to Australia?"

Sheila smiled. "They had married early," she said, "and were still young and adventurous. They had no children – in fact," she added, "I wasn't born until they had settled here and my mother was over forty. I suppose they were too busy making a new life for themselves. Having escaped the Communist regime, they chose to get as far away from it as possible, and Australia looked like the answer – they both spoke English, and my father had engineering qualifications that he found out were acceptable for employment here."

From where she was seated, next to the Baron, Rosemary called out a comment. "They would have been surprised to find when they arrived, back in the 1920's, that Australia – then – had a thriving Communist Party!" she exclaimed.

"Yes, they were surprised," Sheila replied. "But of course they kept themselves scrupulously apart from politics."

"Instead of that, they would have been busy," said Grace, nodding, "establishing themselves in a new country. I don't envy them – having to make that long journey, and then having to find somewhere to live when they arrived here."

"Oh," said Sheila, "they still had the remains of the Radislavsky jewels. That was a stroke of luck. My mother told me how they managed to smuggle them across the border, when they got safely into Romania."

"Surely that would have been a great risk to take," exclaimed Grace.

"Indeed it was," said Sheila. "But when they left Moscow, in the middle of the night, my mother had thoughtfully taken with her a loaf of bread from the kitchen. They had eaten half of it on the way to the border, and there was still half of it left."

Jake was fascinated by the story. "How could that have possibly helped!" he exclaimed. "Surely the border guards wouldn't have been impressed by half a loaf of bread?"

Sheila laughed. "It was my mother's idea," she said. "She got my father to plunge his hand into the loaf and take out a handful of the bread. Then she pressed into the hole the necklace, the earrings and the shoulder pin. And then," she concluded, "they replaced the fistful of bread and pressed it down to make it look natural."

"How clever!" exclaimed Grace. "And it obviously worked!"

"It did indeed," said Sheila. "No x-ray machines at the border in those days. The earrings paid for their voyage to Australia, and the necklace – which they didn't sell until they arrived here – was enough to pay off a substantial amount of the money they needed to buy their first house."

"And the shoulder pin?" Grace enquired.

"It survived," Sheila smiled, "and I'm wearing it tonight." She pointed to her shoulder, where the diamond and ruby brooch gleamed.

Something like a light seemed to go on in Jake's

head. He suddenly had a kind of flash of imagination and knew that he was getting the inspiration he needed for another story. "Maybe called 'The Ruby Brooch'?" he wondered to himself. He looked down the table to where Hugh and Cassie were deep in conversation. Yes, he thought, they really like each other. For a moment, the present scene seemed to melt away and it was as though he was looking down a long corridor – something like a telescope but showing at the end, Hugh and Cassie not as they were now, but as they might be in the future – in formal clothes, with Cassie holding what looked like a bunch of flowers – I'm seeing a wedding, he thought. Then he knew – they were already beginning to fall in love with each other.

It was as simple as that. He felt joy flooding through his consciousness. "I've not only got a brother," he said to himself, "but I'll be getting a sister too." For a moment he felt overwhelmed with emotion, then quickly returned his mind to the present. Grace was leaning across the tale and speaking to Nigel Tremayne.

"Nigel," she said, in her quiet voice, "thanks to Sheila – and Rosemary too, of course – we have all had a remarkable experience tonight. As well," she said, turning to Sheila, "a delicious dinner."

Sheila laughed. "Just the first course, so far," she said, "there'll be another to follow soon."

"I know that in my own case," said Grace, looking fondly across the table to where Cassie sat with Hugh, "I couldn't be happier to have learned what you and Rosemary have revealed to me. And," she added, I think that Cassie feels the same."

Sheila pondered briefly before replying. "Sometimes," she said, "the truth hurts. But, in the long run, whatever hurt it might inflict on us, that is healthier for us than denying whatever reality lies at the heart of whatever version of the truth we have chosen to believe instead."

Jake noticed an unusual expression on Nigel's face. He could tell that Nigel wanted to make a response to what Sheila had just said but was struggling to find out how to say it. Grace noticed it too.

"Nigel," she said, "everyone here tonight has had an illumination of their life story. Jake and Hugh – they found themselves to be brothers. Cassie and myself – "she smiled across the table at Cassie, who gave her an equally warm smile in return. "Even the – the Radislavskys," she continued, "to use the description they go by" – she gestured down to the end of the table – "we heard from them a story that they are obviously not used to telling."

"I can tell what you're thinking," Nigel replied. "You haven't heard anything from me. That is true. And there is a reason for it."

Grace looked across to Nigel, clearly sympathetic to what she saw as his predicament. "If it's too much," she said gently, "then I'm sure no-one will insist." She glanced at Sheila, as though seeking confirmation of what she had just said. But the look on Sheila's face said otherwise. Although she paused before speaking,

Jake was sure that she knew something about Nigel's reticence. And when she did speak, although her voice was as firm and definite as usual, there was a hint of pain in her tone.

"It's about Paul – isn't it," she said. "My late son."

Nigel bowed his head as he replied. "It is," he said.

Sheila also looked down for a moment, as though offering a silent prayer. Then she looked up at Nigel. "I do not know everything," she said to him. "Please be kind enough to tell me."

Jake was moved by the look of desolation that showed so plainly on Nigel's face. He felt that he wanted to echo Grace's remark – to tell Nigel that his story could remain his secret. But he also knew that Sheila was determined to hear it. As though clearing the way for Nigel to begin, she started to give some details of her own life.

"As I've mentioned," she began, "I was born later than usual in my mother's life, and an only child. I don't think my parents spoiled me, but as a child I was given a very strong impression of the Russian background of my family. I knew that there were privileges and possessions that we had lost and that we were embracing a culture that was different from that background."

By this time, Sheila had captured the attention of those further down the table. Even the Radislavskys, Jake noticed, were both listening.

"I suppose," Sheila went on, "it made me what

you could call a bit choosy about who I went out with, when I left school and started to have a social life. There were plenty of parties – we were still in that sort of post-war euphoria that followed the end of the war in Europe and the surrender of Japan in the Pacific. And there were plenty of returned soldiers – war heroes, in my imagination – who were unattached and keen to have a good time now that the fighting was over. And one of them became my husband." She paused. "He was a good man," she said, "and my parents approved. He had fought in New Guinea after the Japanese army had invaded and bombs were being dropped here on Sydney. But with all that in the past, in my mind the future looked rosy. We had a quiet wedding and started married life in a flat that my parents had been able to afford to give us as a wedding present." Sheila paused again, and her face showed a mixture of emotions.

"I soon became pregnant," she continued. "But motherhood didn't bring me the joy I expected it to. When my son – Paul – was only eight months old, my husband suddenly died. The doctor who attended him described the cause simply as heart failure. But to my mind, there were causes that definitely contributed – experiences in the front line of the war had left him with permanent anxiety, inability to sleep soundly because of recurring nightmares, and panic attacks that seemed to be caused by nothing in particular." She paused. "In a way," she said, "my life also ended then – at least, the life I had expected to have."

Grace had been following every word of Sheila's story with an intensity that showed her own feeling for what Sheila had been describing. Jake, as he studied the unspoken link between the speaker and the listener, remembered that Grace had spoken earlier – during what he had filed away in his memory as the "getting to know you" session – she had spoken about her recent widowhood. Three years ago, he recalled her saying that. That would be why, he thought, they have this sort of unspoken understanding between them. And he could tell that each of them understood the relationship that it had created for them. They were women who had both loved, and had both lost.

When Grace spoke, he knew that the question she asked was born of her own experience. "What did you do?" she asked.

"The decision was simple," Sheila replied. "I needed an income, and to be able to get one, I needed a marketable skill. So I found a course that I thought I could cope with – it was called 'Business Management' as I recall – and completed it, after which I found a job with the firm I stayed with for the rest of my working life – until I retired, and became a member of this Club to compensate for the change."

Nigel looked up, a brief smile amending his previous expression.

"That's why my mother joined, too!" he exclaimed. "After she retired."

"We were good friends, your mother and I," Sheila said, "and shared many experiences of some of the messes that men seem to get themselves into when they try to run a business."

"Hah!" exclaimed the voice of the Baroness, from the end of the table. "And what women have to fix up," she said, giving the Baron a meaningful glance.

Rosemary, sitting next to the Baron, intervened. "Let's not go there," she said. "Or," she added, in what was obviously an attempt to lighten the conversation, "we might be here all night."

Her remark didn't seem to have the desired effect on the Baron. He turned to her, his moustache seeming to bristle as he exclaimed, "Madame. You do men an injustice. Men have always been at the service of women."

"Hah!" crowed the Baroness, from her seat opposite. "Too many women I think. Too many fascinations," she added, in a tone that suggested that she had spoken the last word on the matter and the subject was now closed.

At the head of the table, Sheila restored order. "Let's not argue," she said. "After all, we are all human – we each have our own capabilities as well as our own faults. And," she added, "I think that it's the combination of these that shape our own experiences. As I hope tonight might have reminded us."

Rosemary gave Sheila a significant glance. "It's reminded nearly all of us," she said, "but I think there is one last story that we haven't heard yet." As she said this, she nodded towards where Nigel sat. Obviously, she meant him.

To Jake's surprise, Sheila didn't follow up Rosemary's hint. Instead, she said, "I think it's time we asked for the second course. Rosemary, would you mind ringing the bell?"

As Rosemary got up to go to the intercom, Jake noticed the look on Nigel's face. The weariness there, thought Jake, showed just how deeply Nigel's experience – whatever it was – had affected him. Perhaps, Jake wondered, if he told his story, that might be a release for him. His thoughts were interrupted by the voice of the Baroness.

"And what, please, is second course?" she was enquiring.

CHAPTER 11

Nigel's Story

Soon the maids had cleared the empty soup bowls, and another trolley was wheeled in, this time holding covered dinner plates. An enticing aroma could be detected.

"Beef Stroganoff!" Sheila declared, as the maids began serving the table, whipping the covers off the plates as they did so.

"Another Russian dish!" said Grace admiringly.

"Well, it really belongs to the whole world, now," said Sheila. "Ever since the then Count Stroganoff's chef won some international competition with his recipe. Back in the nineteenth century, I think."

"Pah!" exclaimed the Baroness. "Just a Frenchman. He just copy what Russians cook since time began. Everyone," she stressed, "everyone, all know how to make."

"That may be," said Sheila, "but he obviously put his own touch to it. As my mother did. This is her recipe, which I persuaded our chef to use instead of the one he usually uses."

"Well, thank you for doing that," said Hugh, who had just had his first taste. "It's delicious!"

"I must learn how to do it," Cassie said, looking at Hugh. "Since you like it so much," she added. Jake smiled happily to himself as he heard her say this. Something is going on there, he thought to himself – I just know it.

Grace noticed that Nigel was slow to do anything with the meal in front of him. It looked as though he didn't have an appetite, despite the enjoyment all the others seemed to be having as they tasted their Stroganoff. "Do try it, Nigel," she said quietly to him across the table. "It's really nice."

Nigel laid down his fork on his plate. "There is something I have to tell first," he said. He looked at Sheila and smiled sadly. "I will start at the beginning," he said to her.

Sheila replied to his statement. "Perhaps I should first tell you something. Something about Paul that I haven't mentioned before." She paused briefly.

"There are two things," she said. "The first, is that from the age of eight months, Paul grew up without a father. I was never tempted or indeed inclined to marry again."

"Oh," said Nigel earnestly, "Paul knew that. He deeply appreciated how you had provided for him. He loved you, deeply," Nigel said, "I'm sure of it."

"Thank you for saying that," said Shiela.

By now a hush had settled over the table, as all the others began to realise that a story that was of considerable significance to both Nigel and Sheila was about to begin. It was Sheila who started.

"Doing that business course," she said, "meant that I couldn't look after my baby all the time while I had to attend classes as well. So I had to find a suitable girl to do it for me until I could get home again in the afternoon. And that was hard," she said. "After the war, being a nursemaid was not a popular occupation. But I advertised in the local paper, and eventually found someone who I thought would be suitable."

Grace was following Sheila's story with obvious sympathetic interest. "And she didn't work out?" she asked.

"Far from it," Sheila replied. "Every afternoon, when I opened the front door, I could hear Paul begin to cry. I would rush in, to find the girl holding him and comforting him. Every afternoon. And yet," she continued, "on the weekends – Saturdays and Sundays, when I didn't have classes to attend – he was always placid in the afternoons. I began to experience guilt, feeling that I was a bad mother, and that he must somehow feel that on weekdays I was abandoning him, and that was why he cried every afternoon."

"That doesn't sound likely," said Grace.

"As it turned out, it wasn't," said Sheila. "One afternoon I had a cancelled class, the teacher was away sick or something. So I hurried home early. As I opened the front door, I could hear the girl rushing from whatever she was doing in the kitchen into the nursery. I got there just after she had picked Paul up from his cot – in time to see her pinching his legs, making him cry out as he hadn't been doing before."

"So she was the cause," said Grace. She looked thoughtful. "Probably trying to justify her position," she said. "She wanted you to think that she could soothe the child in a way you couldn't. How stupid. And how cruel."

"I didn't stop to think what her motive might have been," said Sheila, "I sacked her on the spot. And missed ten days of the course I was doing, while I tried to find a replacement."

"I hope you found someone better," Grace said.

"Well," said Sheila, "she was certainly better at looking after Paul. I gradually began to trust her with him, and he seemed to respond well to her. But in the long run, she had to go too."

Cassie had listened with increasing interest to

Sheila's story. Now she asked the question, "Why?".

Sheila laughed. "My parents had brought me up to not place too much value on material things," she replied. "After all, in leaving behind their life in Russia they had lost so much, and I suppose that had taught them to recognise that love is the only real power. As opposed to a desire for possessions. They certainly loved each other, and our little family was secure in its circle of emotional warmth. But, as it happened," she continued, "when my husband and I announced our engagement, a dear friend – a girl I'd gone to school with – gave us a little set of silver dessert spoons as an engagement present. I always used them but one day I could only find four of them, instead of the usual six. I asked – Beverley, I think her name was – if she'd seen the others but she said no. Then, the next week, as she was preparing to leave for the day, I came upon her putting two of the remaining four into her knapsack. For a moment I didn't know what to do. Then, I said, very quietly, "just put those back in the drawer where you found them, please Beverley." She gave me such a surly look that I said, straight out, "did you already take the other two?""

Jake was fascinated. "She was stealing them!" he exclaimed.

"She was," said Sheila. "But there wasn't a trace of shame or embarrassment. All she said was 'I didn't think you'd miss them'. She just walked off and never came back. But this time I was ready – I'd secured a place for Paul in the local pre-kindergarten creche, and that's where he went until he was old enough to start school."

Grace had now begun to steer the conversation. She looked across the table, to where Nigel was still struggling to look as though he was enjoying his meal, as everyone else was. She realised that if he was to tell his story, he needed to be prompted. "You couldn't have met Paul at school, Nigel," she said. "It would have been later, I think."

Jake was particularly interested in the way Nigel responded. The suave businessman who had coped so adroitly with tonight's unexpected situation seemed to have been replaced by a nervous middle-aged man looking as though he didn't know how to begin to tell the story that everyone was waiting to hear from him. Jake wanted to help him. "Do you remember," he asked across the table, "where you met him – Paul – for the first time?"

This seemed to unlock Nigel's fund of memories. "Yes of course" he replied." It was at University – during Orientation Week. I'd just come back from London with my parents, and my father had requested my school' – Nigel turned slightly to look down to where the Baron was sitting – "our school," he corrected himself, "to send my matriculation results to Australia. So I was accepted into the faculty of Business Studies."

"Hah!" cried the Baron. "After school I went straight to Monaco. To do real useful business," he emphasised, "not studies of imaginary business." It looked as though the Baron was getting ready to have much more to say on the subject.

To Jake's surprise, it was Ludmilla who interrupted him. Wagging her finger, she said "Shush Ivan. We want to hear. From him," she pointed up towards Nigel, "not from you."

"Please go on, Nigel," said Grace.

"I'd done a bit of rowing at school," Nigel commenced, "so I looked up the University rowing club and went along to their Orientation Week display to find out what they offered. The guy at the information desk asked me if I'd ever done any kayaking. I said I'd tried it out and would be interested in getting more practice. That's when the chap standing next to me said. "I would too!"

"And that was Paul – wasn't it," said Sheila.

"Yes," said Nigel. "That was Paul. We hit it off right away and agreed to practice together twice a week. So that's how our friendship developed – out on the water."

"Kayaking," said Grace. "That's like rowing, isn't it."

Nigel's face lightened, as though he might have almost smiled. "I don't think that rowing is quite the right word," he said. "If you use a two-man kayak, it's an intense teamwork paddling exercise. You use paddles. And fortunately, we had complimentary physiques and we both had a good sense of rhythm." He paused, as though recalling their training sessions. "We decided we'd train for the annual regatta," he continued, "so we never missed a practice session."

"Even in the winter?" asked Jake.

"Even then," Nigel replied.

"Please tell us more," said Sheila. Jake couldn't help noticing the look on her face. It had the bleak appearance of someone eagerly looking at something that had once been appetising. He tried to lighten the shadows of sadness that seemed to have come over the conversation. "How did you go in the regatta?" he asked Nigel.

"The regatta?" said Nigel. "We never made it," he said sadly.

Sheila's businesslike self seemed to reassert itself. "The regatta," she said. "That would have been scheduled for October, wouldn't it."

"Yes," said Nigel, "when the weather has definitely turned to spring, and the annual exams are still far enough off to not have become a worry."

"But before that," said Sheila, in a voice that was fully controlled and showed no trace of what Jake knew she must have felt in having to say it, "my son took his own life."

A silence fell for several moments. Then Sheila spoke again. "I have puzzled over it so many times. But I cannot – I cannot come to an understanding. Why did he do that? He could have had so much life ahead of him." She shook her head sadly, then spoke again to

Nigel. "I'll have to confess to you, Nigel. It was your late mother who told me that you were friends with Paul. One of the reasons I asked you here this evening, to be part of this gathering, was the hope that – somehow – you could be persuaded to help me find an answer to that question."

Nigel looked up. "For many years," he said, "I have asked myself the same question."

"And still you have no answer?" asked Sheila.

"The only answer I have found," said Nigel, "is one which it's hard for me to accept – difficult to believe. Something that I don't want to believe."

"Can you say what it is?" asked Sheila.

Nigel looked straight into Sheila's face. Jake noticed that he had gone pale, as though experiencing a great strain as he pushed away the plate in front of him. Obviously, Jake thought, he didn't want anything more to eat. Or perhaps, couldn't eat more because of how he felt.

Nigel took a deep breath and started to speak. "As we got to know each other through the training sessions," he began, "Paul and I became friends. Best friends, I suppose you could say. I certainly appreciated his company. Occasionally, when we could afford it, we went out and had a drink together at one of the local bars. But," Nigel went on, "I was also getting to know a girl from one of my classes, and taking her out a bit too. And whenever I went out for a drink with Paul after one of those times, he wanted me to give him a full description of what we'd done together." Nigel paused. "Even what happened when I'd said goodnight to her. It was – sort of like he was living through me, wanting to have my experiences rather than his own. At least," Nigel added, "that's how I looked at it – after."

A brief glance round the table told Jake that everyone else also understood what Nigel meant by using the word "after".

"That last training session we had," Nigel continued, "it was a glorious September afternoon and we'd clocked up an improved speed over the distance we were training for. So we were feeling pretty chuffed. Or at least I was. I remember, we were standing at the edge of the water, letting the wavelets wash over our bare feet. I just wanted Paul to know how I felt about training with him. So I said, something like, that I was lucky we got on so well, and that he was a really good friend and a great team-mate." The expression on Nigel's face seemed to darken.

"That's when he turned to me and said – I still remember the words – 'Nigel, you are my only friend'. Then he threw his arms around me, started to give me a hug, and whispered into my ear, 'I want to be your lover'."

There was a shocked silence all round the table.

"I just froze," said Nigel. "There was no misunderstanding what he meant. I know I said something, I don't know what it was, but he pulled away from me – I can still see the look of hurt in his eyes. All I could think of doing was to behave as though what had just happened, hadn't happened at all. I said something like 'come on, let's get Hippolyta back to the boatshed.' We'd christened the kayak we used Hippolyta," he explained.

"The woman warrior goddess," said Cassie.

"That's right," said Nigel. "It was Paul who gave her the name. I just went along with it. Anyway, we paddled back to the boatshed – and instead of both of us storing Hippolyta together, as we usually did, Paul just – he just went off. He didn't say anything. I suppose he caught the first bus that came along. He hadn't even stored his paddle, I had to do that too." Nigel looked up. Something of his usual control seemed to have come back into his face. "That was the last time I saw him," he concluded.

It seemed as though there was nothing anyone could say. Sheila stretched out her hand and rested it lightly on Nigel's. She looked as though she wanted to say something but couldn't. It was Grace who spoke.

"That must be a burden that you have carried ever since," she said quietly to Nigel.

Nigel looked at Grace. "I suppose that's right," he said slowly. "I guess – I don't know – maybe I blamed myself for not understanding him. All I know is, the – the sadness of it has never really gone." He looked appealingly at Sheila. "I'm – I'm sorry," he stammered. "I'm sorry that whatever I said to him didn't tell him how much I valued his friendship – even if his sense of our friendship was – I don't know -- somehow different from mine."

Sheila smiled; but the look in her eyes told Jake just how she must be feeling. "You've blamed yourself ever since, haven't you," she said. "But it wasn't your fault. Oh no. I know what the guilt trip is like. I also blamed myself – for being a bad mother – for not having the capacity to understand my own son – for lacking whatever it was that he needed from me – for not even knowing what it was that he needed – the list is endless."

The poignancy of Nigel's story, and the effect it had obviously created in their hostess, seemed to have changed the whole atmosphere of the gathering. It was Rosemary who realised that it was necessary to lighten the mood. "Time has moved on," she said.

Privately, Jake thought, how does that help things. But then he thought of all the remarkable stories the night had brought to light; and as he was busy with these thoughts, Rosemary added, "I think, for all of us, tonight has worked out to have been an emotional trip none of us ever expected to take. Perhaps we deserve to summon the pudding." She got up from her seat and went to the intercom.

Lifting the receiver, she spoke to Rita. "Rita," she said into the mouthpiece, "ask them to bring in the pavlova."

The effect on the Baroness was electric. "Pavlova!" she exclaimed, in a tone that seemed to bristle with disapproval. "Is not Russian," she pronounced.

"That's right, it isn't," agreed Rosemary cheerfully. "But it was invented, in New Zealand actually, as a tribute to Anna Pavlova the famous Russian ballerina. So tonight, we'll finish our dinner with a celebration of the link between the old world and the new."

The maids had come in and were already clearing the dinner plates and serving everyone with their dessert. Jake, as he picked up his spoon to commence, couldn't help wondering what would happen when this extraordinary dinner would at last be over. And as he began to enjoy his pavlova, he found his imagination wildly brimming with ideas.

CHAPTER 12

An Ending - And A Beginning

As everyone was finishing their dessert, Rosemary called for attention. From where she sat, next to the Baron, she looked up towards Sheila at the head of the table. "On behalf of Sheila and myself," she said, "I want to thank everyone who has come tonight in response to the invitation you received. Sheila and I gave this dinner a lot of thought, and we decided to send the invitation anonymously in the hope that it would intrigue you enough to bring you along."

Jake wasn't surprised that Grace began to reply to this. He could tell, as she started to speak, that she was taking particular care to choose her words carefully. "Nothing," she commenced, "could have prepared me for the experience I have had tonight. What it has proved to me is that if you love someone – even if that person is taken away from you –the love you have for them never dies."

At the head of the table, Sheila spread her hands widely in front of her. "Love," she said, "is the only reality. We may delude ourselves with accumulated wealth, with the adulation of those who for whatever reason envy us, for the ambitions we harbour because they bolster our self-esteem, but in the long run, if we deny love, we deny life."

Looking across the table, Jake could tell how deeply this statement affected Nigel.

"I know you're right," Nigel said soberly, "but sometimes love is not always possible."

"It may not be possible to express," said Grace. "But it is still there."

"Then why do people fall out of love?" Jake asked.

In the silence that followed, he wondered if anyone would offer an answer. Soon, one came, and from an unexpected source. It was the Baroness.

"In Monaco," she said, "many love affairs. First this one, then that one. Fascinations," she pronounced, fixing the Baron with a steely gaze. "But not love," she explained, flourishing her table napkin. "Fascinations!" she stressed, shifting her gaze to take in the whole table. Her eyes rested on Jake. "Fascinations, not love. So who can fall out of love if have never fallen in?"

"You mean," said Jake, "that people may think they're in love, but aren't really?"

"Oh, that happens such a lot," said Cassie, looking first at Jake and then down the table towards Ludmilla, as though answering her. "I have so many friends who've had break-ups. And it seems to happen," she said, "when they realise something about the other person that they weren't aware of before. Something – I don't know – that changes the way they feel about them."

"And that proves," said Hugh, smiling as he said it, "that you shouldn't let yourself get serious about someone until you know them really well."

Grace nodded. "And sometimes that takes time," she said, "but sometimes they both just know it – instantly."

"Or think they do," said Nigel. "But it turns out to be a delusion," he added quietly.

Sheila looked thoughtfully at both Grace and Nigel. "I think you two should talk more about this," she said. "Grace, maybe Nigel could come in to the club if you were to invite him for afternoon tea sometime."

Grace smiled. "That would be nice," she said, "except that I can't do it as I'm not a member."

"Oh!" said Sheila. "Let's fix that. Rosemary chairs the club's membership committee and they're having their meeting next Tuesday morning. Rosemary!" she called, "I'm proposing Grace for club membership. Can you handle it?"

"As good as done and dusted," Rosemary called back.

"So!" said Sheila. "We might be able to have another little meeting – over afternoon tea next Tuesday. Those who would be free to come," she added.

"Hah!" said the Baroness. "Impossible!" she added, speaking the word with a French accent.

"Do you have other plans, Ludmilla?" Rosemary enquired.

"Cruise," said Ludmilla enigmatically.

"Oh yes," said Rosemary. "When I was investigating your movements, so that Sheila and I could set a date for this dinner that would include you, I remember that the cruise ship you came to Sydney on was due to continue to New Zealand, and dock here again next Saturday on its return voyage to Europe. So – you have decided to return?"

"We," said Ludmilla, heavily stressing the word, "have decided."

Something of Nigel's polished manner had returned to him. "Won't you have difficulty," he asked, "in getting a double stateroom?"

A hint of embarrassment briefly crossed Ludmilla's face and was gone again. "It is done," she said tersely; then, to the Baron, "king size bed, private balcony. You will enjoy."

"How on earth did you manage to do that!"

exclaimed Nigel.

"Ah," said the Baroness. "On voyage here I cultivate Purser. He agree to hold spare cabin for my return."

"So you knew you were going to forgive your husband!" exclaimed Grace. "Even before he rang you from Monaco!" If Grace expected a reply to her observation, it did not happen. The Baron fixed Ludmilla with what for him was a look of deep enquiry.

"This man," he said, "this – Purser. This man with cabins. I hope he is not for you a fascination."

Much to Jake's surprise, Ludmilla smiled at this. "You know, Ivan, I do not have fascinations," she said. "Instead, I have one love. That is you."

Sheila and Rosemary exchanged glances. It was almost as though they were celebrating a dual achievement, Jake thought. The Baron reached for Ludmilla's hand. "I am the lucky man," he said simply.

Somehow this reconciliation signalled the end of the evening. As Hugh rose from his chair, he said "I've offered to see Cassie home."

"I'll ring you, Aunt Grace," said Cassie. As she and Hugh moved towards the door, they both offered thanks for the evening. Jake watched them go. Ludmilla and Ivan were also on the move. "We go to my hotel," Ludmilla explained. Ivan bowed to both Sheila and Rosemary and they quickly left the dining room.

"And you, Jake?" asked Rosemary. "Has tonight

given you a new direction?"

Jake beamed. He felt a familiar excitement. "I'm going home to begin a story," he said excitedly. "I just want to sort it out in my head first – but I think, if you don't mind, I might set it in a women's club – just like this one – with a whole lot of people who start out as strangers and then have a mysterious adventure that changes their lives forever."

Sheila laughed. "A mystery that you will have to solve," she said.

"Yes," said Jake. "A mystery at the Hippolyta Club. I might call it that." He said goodnight to those who remained.

"H'm," he thought to himself as he went down the corridor, left the Minerva Club and waited for the lift to come to level 11 in response to his summons. "Not a bad title," he thought. In his mind, a story began to unfold – just as the street under his feet began to lead him unfailingly towards his lodgings and the computer keyboard that was waiting for him there -- and for the story he would begin to tell on it.

Frank Sutherland Davidson